Elizabeth was so nervous as she stood next to Jessica at the wedding that she could feel her hands trembling. *Please behave yourself*, Elizabeth silently begged her twin. *Don't spoil this moment for Sue!* This could be one of the last happy moments of Sue's life.

Elizabeth turned her gaze toward Jeremy and saw something that caused her heart to constrict. He wasn't looking at Sue! He was gazing into the eyes of Jessica! *How could he?! At his own wedding?!* She looked at Jessica and saw that she was staring at him as well. Elizabeth knew her sister well enough to know that she was trying to send some sort of terrible message to Jeremy.

Elizabeth didn't think her nerves could take much more of this. Suddenly, Elizabeth sensed Jessica's body tense up. *Hurry up! Hurry up!* Elizabeth felt herself break into a sweat.

"If any man or woman knows of any any reason why this couple should not be joined as one under the realm of god, speak now or forever hold your peace."

Elizabeth held her breath and closed her eyes.

LEFT AT
THE ALTAR

Written by
Kate William

Created by
FRANCINE PASCAL

BANTAM BOOKS
NEW YORK • TORONTO • LONDON • SYDNEY • AUCKLAND

RL 6, age 12 and up

LEFT AT THE ALTAR

A Bantam Book / August 1994

Sweet Valley High® is a registered trademark of Francine Pascal
Conceived by Francine Pascal
Produced by Daniel Weiss Associates, Inc.
33 West 17th Street
New York, NY 10011
Cover art by Bruce Emmett

ISBN: 0-553-56230-4

Published simultaneously in the United States and Canada

Bantam Books are published by Bantam Books, a division of Bantam
Doubleday Dell Publishing Group, Inc. Its trademark, consisting of the
words "Bantam Books" and the portrayal of a rooster, is Registered in
U.S. Patent and Trademark Office and in other countries. Marca
Registrada. Bantam Books, 1540 Broadway, New York, New York 10036.

PRINTED IN THE UNITED STATES OF AMERICA

OPM   0 9 8 7 6 5 4 3 2 1

To Alice Elizabeth Wenk

Chapter 1

"I've been dreaming of doing this again ever since the last time," Jeremy Randall said to Jessica Wakefield between long, passionate kisses. "I thought I would go crazy if I didn't kiss you again."

"I know. Me too," Jessica said, her heart pounding. "I've been waiting for the moment when we could finally be alone together."

Jessica was happier than she'd ever been. She was kissing Jeremy again, the most gorgeous guy she'd seen in her entire life. Her dream had come true. Jeremy really did care for her. It didn't matter that he was engaged to marry Sue Gibbons, the daughter of Jessica's mother's college roommate. Jessica didn't even care that they were at the engagement party for Sue and Jeremy. The sounds coming from around the Wakefields' house

1

seemed light years away. She felt as if she and Jeremy were the only two people in the world.

Ever since Jessica met Jeremy on the beach, weeks before, she had tried desperately to get him to admit his feelings for her. It was obvious to her, when they kissed on that first day, there was a chemistry between them that happened only once in a lifetime. When they first met, Jessica had no idea that Jeremy was on the verge of getting married to someone else. She just thought he was this magical, blond hunk who had appeared from nowhere to be with her. She had been horrified when she first found out that not only was he engaged, he was engaged to be married to Sue! But now, Jessica knew, not even that mattered. *Like the song says, we were meant to be together.*

"I've been fighting my feelings for you every step of the way, but I realize now that that's impossible," Jeremy said, holding Jessica tightly. "You know what they say. Only the fool thinks he has a choice when it comes to matters of the heart. I guess I was being a fool."

"I knew you felt the same way I did," Jessica said breathlessly. "You had to."

Jessica felt like she could stand in the garden, kissing Jeremy, for the rest of her life. She never wanted to leave his embrace.

"Jeremy! Jeremy!" The sound of Sue's voice wafted through the party crowd, just barely reaching them where they stood concealed behind the rosebushes.

Still, Jessica refused to let go of him. *Maybe it's just as well that Sue finds out the truth about us,* Jessica thought. *This whole engagement is a lie anyway. There's no way he can marry Sue now that he's finally faced his true feelings for me. The sooner she finds out, the better.*

"Jeremy! Jeremy!"

"This is a great party," Enid Rollins said to Elizabeth Wakefield. Enid was Elizabeth's best friend, after her identical twin sister, Jessica.

Elizabeth stood at the refreshment table staring off into space while Enid popped another California roll into her mouth. "This sushi spread is totally awesome," Enid said between bites.

"Earth to Elizabeth," Enid said, waving a hand in front of Elizabeth's face. "What planet are you on?"

"Oh, sorry," Elizabeth said absently. "Did you say something?"

"I was just talking about the food. Your parents really went all out for this party for Sue," Enid said.

"I know. Have you seen Jessica?" Elizabeth asked with a worried expression on her face.

"I saw her dancing with Jeremy about ten minutes ago," Enid said.

"That's what I was afraid of," Elizabeth muttered. *And I haven't seen them since.* Elizabeth was horrified but not surprised that her sister would be sneaking off with Jeremy at Sue's engagement party. *Couldn't she just show a little restraint on this one occasion?* Elizabeth thought. Elizabeth was accustomed to Jessica's outrageous behavior, but getting involved with an almost-married man really took the cake.

For the thousandth time, Elizabeth marveled at the fact that they were even related, much less twins. True, on the outside, the twins were completely identical. They both had golden-blond hair, green-blue eyes the color of the Pacific Ocean, and dimples on their left cheeks. But that's where the similarities ended. Elizabeth was every bit as popular as her sister and liked to have as much fun as the next person, but she had a serious streak. She liked to spend her free time reading, and during the school year, working on *The Oracle*, the Sweet Valley High newspaper where she was a writer. She had plans to be a professional writer when she got older.

Jessica, on the other hand, was more interested in clothes, boys, parties, and gossip than in school. Jessica was the first to admit that she was boy crazy, but this latest infatuation—or whatever it was—worried Elizabeth. Jessica had jumped into this thing with Jeremy with her eyes closed—the usual way she did things—but Elizabeth was afraid this time her sister was in way over her head.

This won't go any farther if I have anything to do with it, Elizabeth thought as she walked out to the garden. Elizabeth was thinking about all the people who would be affected by Jessica's actions. Sue would be devastated by Jeremy's betrayal, and Elizabeth's parents would be hurt as well. And no matter what the outcome would be, Elizabeth knew that Jessica would suffer a terrible heartache. She was determined to do anything to keep her sister from being hurt the way she herself had been hurt after she'd fallen in love with Luke in London just a few weeks earlier.

"What do you think you're doing?" Elizabeth exclaimed as she pulled her sister away from Jeremy as they kissed in the backyard behind some hedges.

"I think it's pretty obvious what we're doing," Jessica said crossly. "The question is, what do you think *you're* doing?"

"May I remind you that there are seventy people in that house, including your fiancée, Jeremy, who are all here to celebrate your wedding," Elizabeth scolded them. She wiped the lipstick off Jeremy's mouth and pulled the shoulder strap up on Jessica's sleeveless dress. Elizabeth looked all around to make sure nobody else had seen what she'd seen.

"Elizabeth's right," Jeremy muttered guiltily.

5

"Your parents were really generous, giving this party for Sue and me . . ."

"I don't care if she's right or not," Jessica said, her face turning red with anger. "The point is that what we're doing is *our* business."

"No, in this case it's not just your business," Elizabeth said hotly. "It's Sue's business, and Mom and Dad's business, and the business of every guest inside that house who brought a gift for Jeremy and Sue."

"You know, ever since you got back from London you've been a total control freak. Maybe you should go upstairs to your room and read some more pop-psychology and figure out why you're so concerned with everyone's problems except your own," Jessica said.

Elizabeth felt as if she was about to cry. Maybe she *was* being a little bossy but it was only out of love for her sister. She didn't want what had happened to her in London to happen to Jessica. Not only had her heart been broken, but she'd become totally mistrustful of men. Luckily, Todd was still on vacation when she got back, so she'd figured she had some time to get herself together before he returned to Sweet Valley. She'd immersed herself in several different self-help books that talked about how to stay strong and hold on to one's self in a relationship. She'd also joined a primal woman seminar that had enabled her to start feeling

6

stronger. She was trying to use that new-found strength to keep her sister from falling into that abyss of heartache she knew too well.

Elizabeth looked at her sister, who was looking back at her with pure resentment. *I just don't want you to get hurt, Jess*, she wanted to say. *I don't want you to lose control the way I did in London.*

"There you are!" Sue said excitedly to Jeremy as she appeared around the rosebushes. "It looks like you're having your own party out here with these two pretty girls." Sue walked up to the three of them and put her arms around Elizabeth and Jessica's waists.

Elizabeth felt her stomach do a back flip. *Poor Sue is definitely going to suspect something.* "Hey, Sue," Elizabeth said in an overly cheerful and excited voice. "We were just out here, um, looking for some more flowers to bring in the house. But, there are just roses out here, and we already have enough roses, so, well, I guess we can go back inside now." Elizabeth was talking so quickly that she barely even knew what she was saying.

"Well, that was sweet of you guys," Sue said, smiling. "Jeremy, honey, I want you to come and meet Father Bishop. He wants to get to know us better. He *is* going to marry us, after all."

"That's right!" Elizabeth said quickly, looking pointedly at Jessica. "He's going to marry you, be-

7

cause you are getting married, since you're engaged and all. You two lovebirds just go on ahead, and Jessica and I will be right in." *It's a good thing I got here when I did*, Elizabeth thought as Sue linked arms with Jeremy and kissed him on the cheek before taking him inside to meet Father Bishop. *But if I have to go through any more close calls like that I'm going to have an ulcer at the age of sixteen!*

Jessica's heart sank when Jeremy went with Sue into the house. "Don't say anything," Jessica said curtly to Elizabeth.

"Don't say anything about what?" Elizabeth asked.

"Anything about Jeremy going inside with Sue," Jessica said, gazing listlessly in the direction of the house. "He has no choice. I know he'd rather be with me, but it's his duty to go with Sue. Poor baby." Jessica let out a heavy sigh.

"Poor baby!" Elizabeth repeated incredulously. "What about poor Sue?"

"I'm not in the mood for this now," Jessica said.

"Look, Jess, I don't mean to be bossy, but I just don't see how this situation can end without you getting hurt," Elizabeth said gently. "Not only is he about to marry Sue, he's twenty-three and you're only sixteen. It's a huge age difference. I just don't think you've thought this through."

"Sometimes in life you can't think," Jessica said. "Sometimes you can only feel. What I feel now is that I'm totally crazy about Jeremy, and he's finally admitted that he feels the same way about me. There's nothing you or anybody else can say to change the fact that Jeremy Randall and Jessica Wakefield were meant to be together. So just please leave me in peace."

All Jessica wanted was to be alone and remember every single detail of her last moments with Jeremy before Elizabeth so rudely interrupted them.

"Elizabeth! Jessica!" Mrs. Wakefield called from inside the house. "It's time to make the toasts! Come inside!"

"You go on in," Jessica told Elizabeth as she plopped into one of the lounge chairs by the pool. "I'm going to sit this one out."

"Oh, no, you're not, missy," Elizabeth said, pulling Jessica off the chair. "You're going to wipe that love-stricken expression off your face, march inside that house, and act normal. Jeremy is marrying *Sue*, not *you*, so start facing reality!"

Not if I have anything to do with it, Jessica schemed. Jessica didn't set out to fall in love with a man who was engaged to be married. It just happened that way. *It's not my fault this happened. But now that it has, it's too late to stop our love from running its natural course. And if nature*

9

*needs a little coaxing, then I'll just have to do what-
ever I need to do to keep it moving.*

"I'd like everyone to raise their glass to Jeremy
and Sue," Alice Wakefield said to the guests who
were assembled in the living room. Mrs.
Wakefield was still a beautiful woman and
Elizabeth thought her mother looked more radiant than ever in the pink chiffon dress she was
wearing for the occasion. "I want to wish them
every happiness in the world. I only wish Nancy,
Sue's mother and my college roommate, could be
here tonight to share in this joyful event. I know
Nancy would be thrilled that her beautiful and in-
telligent daughter has found the perfect match.
She would agree with me that not only are they
very much in love with each other, but that they
are truly meant to be together."

"She's wrong," Jessica said under her breath but
loud enough for Elizabeth, who was standing next
to her, to hear. "He and *I* are meant to be together."

Elizabeth didn't know if she was more worried
about Sue or her mother hearing Jessica's outburst.
Elizabeth glanced around the room at the sumptu-
ous spread and all the flowers her mother had ar-
ranged. Mrs. Wakefield had supervised every last
detail of the party. Elizabeth knew that Sue's wedding was super-important to her mother because of
her friendship with Sue's mother. When Nancy

Gibbons died, Mrs. Wakefield had stayed in bed crying for days. Elizabeth knew their mother would be horrified if she found out about Jessica's feelings for Jeremy.

"Shhhhh," Elizabeth commanded nervously to her sister. "Do you want everyone to hear you? I seriously think you're losing all sense of reality."

"I have never had a better sense of reality than I have at this moment," Jessica said as her eyes shone brightly and she looked directly at Jeremy. "I can't remember the last time I ever felt so awake and aware of my feelings. The only thing standing in our way is Sue. Sometimes I wish she would just disappear."

"Jessica, that's a horrible thing to say!" Elizabeth said.

"Well, it's how I feel," Jessica said.

"It's not like this is the first guy you've ever thought you were in love with," Elizabeth said as she looked around the room to make sure no one could hear their whispered but urgent conversation. "Just a few weeks ago in London you were saying the same thing about Lord Robert Pembroke. And what about poor Sam, and Aaron, and the dozens of other guys you've been wildly in love with?"

"Except for Sam, everyone before Jeremy was a child," Jessica said gravely. Sam Woodruff was Jessica's serious boyfriend who had died in a tragic car accident earlier that year. Elizabeth knew that Jessica would always have a special place in her heart for Sam. "*I* was a child. For the first time in my life, I feel like a woman."

"But you're only sixteen," Elizabeth said. "You're still young."

"Stop saying I'm sixteen," Jessica said. "I know how old I am. Age has nothing to do with love. Look at Romeo and Juliet. They were like thirteen or fourteen. They were so in love that they *died* for each other."

"Well, we're not talking about Romeo and Juliet," Elizabeth said. "We're talking about Jessica Wakefield, sixteen-year-old girl with a whole future in front of her, and Jeremy Randall, twenty-three-year-old engaged to marry Sue Gibbons in a couple of weeks. Now, I know you like a challenge and you always want what you can't have. But in this case, you have to think about all the other people involved. This is one competition you have to let go of."

"This isn't about wanting what I can't have," Jessica said. "This is about true love."

Elizabeth stared silently at Jessica. It was true that Elizabeth had heard her sister say that she'd found the man of her dreams hundreds of times in the past. But this time, Jessica was so adamant it scared Elizabeth. She'd never seen Jessica so serious about anything in her life. *What if she re-*

ally is as in love as she says she is? What if this really is the love of her life? Elizabeth worried. She looked across the room at Sue's happy, naive face then back at her sister's serious, lovesick expression. *Even if she is really in love, this can't continue. Too many people would get hurt. Especially my sister.*

"If I could have everybody's attention again," Alice Wakefield said to the guests who were talking excitedly after her toast. "Now my daughters would like to say a few words on behalf of the happy couple."

"Not this daughter," Jessica said loud enough to provoke a poke in the ribs from Elizabeth. "Ouch! You don't honestly expect me to give some speech right now, do you?"

"I guess not," Elizabeth conceded. Elizabeth didn't even know how *she* would manage to say anything halfway convincing, considering the circumstances. What could she say? *Ladies and gentlemen, I'd like to propose a toast to my sister, Jessica, who has fallen in love with Jeremy?*

"Elizabeth? Jessica?" Mrs. Wakefield asked expectantly, smiling in their direction.

Elizabeth glanced at her sister, who looked as if she had lockjaw. Then she took a deep breath. "Ladies and gentlemen," Elizabeth started. She heard her voice shaking. "My sister, Jessica, and I would like to propose a toast to Jeremy and Sue."

13

Elizabeth turned to smile at Jessica to give the impression that this was in fact a shared toast. To Elizabeth's horror, Jessica was running out of the living room and up the stairs.

"Please excuse my sister," Elizabeth said, trying with all her might to force a giggle. "She's not used to drinking champagne."

The laughter that filled the room brought Elizabeth temporary relief and enabled her to get through the rest of her toast.

"As I was saying," Elizabeth continued. "We feel as if Sue is a new sister and that Jeremy will be a new brother. . . ." At that moment Elizabeth heard the sound of a door slamming upstairs.

"What's wrong with you?" Steven Wakefield asked Elizabeth after the toasts were made. Steven was Elizabeth and Jessica's older brother. "You look like you're about to be sick. Don't tell me you've been hitting the champagne, too."

"Yeah, right," Elizabeth said, laughing at the thought. Her brother always had that effect on her. Tall, dark, and handsome, he looked just like their father and always seemed to know what to say to make Elizabeth feel better. This time, though, Elizabeth had the feeling that a little laugh was all he'd be able to get out of her.

"Well, what is it then?" Steven pressed.

Elizabeth wasn't sure if she should tell Steven

about Jessica and Jeremy, but she was worried that it was becoming more than she could handle. And besides, Steven was her brother, and apart from Elizabeth, he knew Jessica better than anyone. Also, Elizabeth knew she could trust him with a secret.

"OK, follow me," Elizabeth said, walking outside to sit by the pool.

"Is it serious?" Steven said, concerned.

"It's about Jessica," Elizabeth said as they were seated at one of the poolside tables. "You have to swear yourself to total secrecy if I tell you," Elizabeth said.

"I swear," Steven said, looking more relaxed. "Let me guess—she's in some kind of mess and you have to get her out of it."

Elizabeth took a sip of her diet soda, swallowed, and then told Steven the whole sordid story.

Steven listened attentively and when Elizabeth was finished he said, "Look, I wouldn't worry about it so much. You know Jessica, she's fallen in love more times than Elizabeth Taylor. It doesn't mean anything."

"This is different," Elizabeth said. "I can't explain it, but she's more serious about Jeremy than she's ever been about anyone. Even Sam!"

"Elizabeth, listen. You're going to make yourself crazy if you try to control Jessica," Steven cautioned as he dipped a tortilla chip into the bowl of

15

guacamole on the table. "Besides, I'm sure this will blow over."

"It's not going to just blow over. Believe me. She's out of control. It's like a love-addiction," Elizabeth said.

"What's 'love addiction'?" Steven asked.

"I've been reading about it in this book called *Love: Addiction and Obsession and How to Overcome It*," Elizabeth explained. "All these women become addicted to men, and it's like a physical disease. Like alcohol or drug addiction."

"You don't need a book to understand Jessica. You just have to look at the way she's been her whole life. And let's say she *is* love-addicted or whatever. There's nothing you can do about it anyway. You're not responsible for Jessica's actions."

"But if it's a disease, like alcoholism or something, she won't be able to help herself," Elizabeth said. "We have to do something to stop her—like a family intervention."

"It's not a disease, Liz," Steven said calmly. "It's a crush or an infatuation. Now, I'm going to go back to the party to snarf down some more sushi and have a good time, and I suggest you do the same thing. Don't worry so much, little sis."

Elizabeth sat alone at the table feeling more desperate than ever. *How can Steven take it so lightly?* Just then, Enid joined her at the table.

"Enid, what am I going to do about Jessica?" Elizabeth wailed.

"You can only be responsible for yourself," Enid said. "And that's hard enough as it is."

"But I have to do something to stop her," Elizabeth cried.

"You know your sister better than anyone, so I don't think I need to remind you that your twin sister always manages to get what she wants," Enid said ominously.

She's right. Jessica does always get what she wants, but this is one time when she just can't and I'm the only person who can make sure of that! Elizabeth was more determined than ever to keep Jeremy and Jessica apart.

Chapter 2

Jessica stood on the beach, her white gown flowing in the breeze. As the sun set behind her, she looked into Jeremy's enormous coffee eyes. "I do," Jeremy said. "I take Jessica Wakefield to be my lawfully wedded bride."

"I now pronounce you husband and wife," Father Bishop said. "You may kiss the bride."

Jeremy pulled Jessica toward him. . . .

Suddenly Jessica woke up. With a sick feeling, she realized that she'd only been dreaming. She wasn't the one marrying Jeremy. Just as she was about to pull the covers back over her head in an attempt to return to her dream, she heard the tapping sound at the window. The sound that had woken her. She sat up and peered outside. She couldn't believe her eyes. "Jeremy!" she shrieked.

She ran to her closet and pulled on a sexy, black backless sundress, brushed her hair, and spritzed herself with her new favorite perfume. She looked at herself in the mirror and liked what she saw. *OK, Jeremy, here I come!*

She tiptoed quickly down the stairs, trying not to make any noise. She was so excited, she could barely breathe. *Maybe he wants to run away and elope*, she fantasized. *Maybe he wants to take me away to a tropical rain forest in the Amazon or wherever rain forests are*. Jessica didn't know that much about rain forests, but she wanted to learn everything she could about them because Jeremy was so passionate about the subject. It was the main focus of his work at Project Nature.

When she saw Jeremy standing against his rented white sports car convertible, wearing a denim jacket and jeans, her heart leapt. *Remain calm*, she told herself. She was afraid she wouldn't be able to speak because of her attraction to Jeremy. She felt her mouth widen in a huge smile. She tried to straighten it out so she wouldn't look overeager, but she couldn't stop smiling.

"I had to come," Jeremy said, holding out his arms. Jessica ran into Jeremy's strong, outstretched arms and burrowed her face in his chest. "I was just dreaming about you," she gushed as he pulled her closer to him. "We were standing on the beach and the sun was setting." She didn't tell him she was dreaming that it was their wedding day. That might be pushing things a little too much.

"Then you must be a mind reader because we're going to see the sun, but it's going to be rising, and we're going to the water, but it's Secca Lake, not the ocean. And most importantly, it won't be a dream," Jeremy said as he kissed her on the top of her head. "It will only feel like one."

Jeremy and Jessica had just pulled away from each other to head for Jeremy's car when Sue appeared from inside the house.

OK, this is it, Jessica thought nervously. *Now Jeremy will tell her everything and this whole business will be finished once and for all*. Jessica's stomach was tied up in knots, but she knew that this was the inevitable confrontation she had been waiting for.

"Jeremy!" Sue exclaimed gleefully. "What a wonderful surprise. I couldn't sleep and I was thinking what a magical sunrise we're about to have. Let's go to Secca Lake and watch it together."

"I was just thinking the same thing," Jeremy said tentatively, looking at Jessica.

"Jessica, you're up awfully early," Sue said.

21

"Let me guess, you've been out all night with Bruce."

Jessica had gotten Bruce Patman, Sweet Valley's richest, cutest, and most obnoxious boy to pretend that he was her date one night so that she could spy on Sue and Jeremy at the Carousel. Ever since then, Sue was convinced that Bruce and Jessica were really boyfriend and girlfriend, and she made constant references to it. "That's right," Jessica said nervously.

"Don't worry, I won't say anything to your parents." Sue smiled.

"Thanks," Jessica said. "I'd appreciate that."

"I'm so glad to see you with Jeremy. And this is a perfect opportunity for you and Jessica to get to know each other better. After all, I feel like we're all family," Sue said sweetly. "And I just noticed for the first time how alike you two look. You really look like you could be brother and sister."

Jessica *had* actually thought about how much they looked like each other. Except for those dark eyes and those gorgeous, well-muscled shoulders, he could almost be her twin. Which only proved further that they were made for each other. *We're each other's perfect other half.* It really irked her, though, to hear Sue say they were like brother and sister. Jeremy's feelings for her were certainly more than brotherly, and Jessica could have stood a little jealousy from Sue instead of this "I'm so glad to see you with Jeremy" business. *If you knew the truth, you wouldn't be so happy about us being together*, Jessica thought. She was dying to blurt out what was really going on, but she knew that if anyone was going to say something it had to Jeremy—he wouldn't want her to find out in any other way. Still, the temptation to say something was overwhelming.

"That's such a cute little dress you're wearing. Jeremy, doesn't Jessica look adorable?"

Cute? Adorable? Jessica hated to be described as being either of those two things. "Cute" was the last thing Jessica wanted Jeremy to think she was.

"We should get going if we want to catch the sunrise," Jeremy said to Sue.

"Jessica, you have to come with us. I won't take no for an answer," Sue said, putting her arm around Jeremy's waist.

"Well, I'm not sure," Jessica started. The idea of watching the sunrise with Jeremy and Sue was more than she could bear. After all, it was supposed to be her own private date with Jeremy.

"Oh, you have to come," Sue insisted. "It'll be fun and Jeremy will be both of our dates."

"I hope we make it there in time for the sunrise," Sue said. "I don't think I've ever seen a beautiful sunrise in New York. That's another reason I think we should move to California."

"You mean you'd give up the stink and grime of the subways to enjoy the beauty of nature out here?" Jeremy joked.

Both Sue and Jeremy laughed and Jessica wanted to sink to the floor of the car. *They have a whole life together in New York that I don't know anything about,* Jessica thought sadly. She was sitting in the backseat while Jeremy and Sue sat in front. *This is just great. I'm supposed to be alone with Jeremy, and I feel like the little sister tagging along on their date.*

Jessica sat right behind the driver's seat. As she looked ahead through the windshield, she caught Jeremy glancing at her in the rearview mirror. Their eyes locked and she realized that they had *their* own special world that nobody else could know about. Jeremy's gaze made Jessica feel better in what was an extremely uncomfortable situation.

"That party your parents gave us last night was so wonderful," Sue gushed, turning around to look at Jessica. "It was great to meet your parents' friends. I can't wait to open all those presents. Didn't you have fun, honey?" Sue asked Jeremy.

"Oh, yeah. It was great," Jeremy said, catching Jessica's gaze again in the mirror.

Say something now about you and me! Jessica wanted to shout to Jeremy. "I was wondering if you had a chance to tell Sue about what we talked about last night," Jessica said, trying to prod him on a little.

"No, not yet," Jeremy murmured as his face turned red.

"Oh, what was that?" Sue asked.

"Nothing," Jeremy said curtly. "Just something about the wedding. We'll talk about it later."

"You two are being awfully secretive," Sue said smiling. "Are you plotting some kind of surprise?"

"Oh, you'll be surprised all right," Jessica said, hoping that Sue would catch the underlying meaning in her suggestive tone. Instead, it seemed to be totally lost on her.

"Just think, baby, we have a whole lifetime of sunrises and sunsets to see together," Sue said, oblivious. "This is just the first of millions to come." She leaned toward Jeremy and planted a big, wet kiss on his mouth. Jessica couldn't help being jealous. Sue *was* a beautiful woman after all, and she and Jeremy had a special bond because of the work they both did for the environment. They had traveled to exotic places together, and Jessica knew how important Jeremy's work was to him. All she'd ever done for the environment was put an occasional soda can in the recycling bins on the street. It took all of her restraint not to simply yank Sue away from Jeremy.

Does he like kissing her? Jessica wondered. It was always possible that he still felt some attraction toward Sue. Watching him kiss her was sheer agony.

"Green light!" Jessica yelled from the backseat, causing Jeremy and Sue to pull apart.

Sue turned around and looked at Jessica as if she'd forgotten she was in the car with them. "I hope you're feeling better, Jessie," Sue said.

"What do you mean?" Jessica asked, cringing at Sue's use of her nickname. "Jessie" sounded juvenile and the only person who could get away with calling her that was Elizabeth.

"The champagne," Sue explained. "I remember when I was about your age and had champagne for the first time. It was a little more than I could handle back then."

"Actually," Jessica started, "it wasn't really *that* long ago that you were my age. I mean, after all, you *are* only two years older than me." Jessica was getting really sick of Sue making such a big deal about their age diffence.

"I guess you're right," Sue conceded. "I guess I just feel older than my age. When my mother died, I felt as if I'd aged about fifteen years. I hope you'll never feel older than your age like I do."

If I'm supposed to feel sorry for her, it's not

26

working, Jessica thought. She watched as Jeremy turned toward Sue and gave her a sympathetic smile. Jessica realized that she couldn't endure watching the sunrise with Sue's cooing and kissing and acting all helpless.

"To tell you the truth," Jessica started as they pulled up to the side of the lake, "I'm still feeling pretty nauseated. Would you mind terribly if we just turned around and went back home?"

Your first sunrise of a lifetime of sunrises will have to wait, Jessica thought as Jeremy turned the car around and headed home. *In fact, you won't ever see any sunrises or sunsets together if I have anything to do with it.*

"Oh, hey guys," Elizabeth said when Jessica, Jeremy, and Sue came into the kitchen in time to have breakfast. Elizabeth, Mr. and Mrs. Wakefield, and Steven were already sitting at the table. Elizabeth gave Jessica a disapproving look that Jessica chose to ignore. "Where have you all been?"

"We just went for an early morning ride to the lake," Sue said.

"I must be losing my hearing," Steven said. "Did you just say that my sister was out for an early morning ride to the lake?"

"Yes, that's what she said," Jessica said hotly.

"That must not have been very romantic having

27

Jessica around as the third wheel," Elizabeth said.

Jessica just glared at Elizabeth.

"Sit down, everyone," Mr. Wakefield said. "I just made a batch of my famous blueberry waffles."

"I love blueberry waffles," Sue enthused. "Jeremy makes delicious waffles himself. That's one of the reasons I fell in love with him."

Jessica looked across the table at Jeremy who was blushing, obviously embarrassed by the way Sue gushed about him.

"Maybe we should have a waffle competition," Mrs. Wakefield said. "In fact, what if during this time before the wedding everyone takes turns making their favorite recipes?"

"That's a great idea," Sue said.

"I hope everyone likes frozen dinners because that's going to be my contribution," Steven said.

"I can't thank you enough for that magnificent party you gave us last night, Aunt Alice and Uncle Ned," Sue said as she smothered the waffles in syrup. "It's a night we'll always remember, and I know how happy it would make my mother to know you're looking out for us."

"It really *was* a great party," Jeremy agreed. "Thanks a million."

Sue took Jeremy's hand and Jessica noticed that Jeremy was squirming in his seat, looking extremely uncomfortable.

"I think I speak for all of us when I say that we

28

feel like the two of you are a part of our family," Mr. Wakefield said. "We're just so happy for you. You're clearly as much in love as Alice and I were when we got married. As much as we still are, I should add. I hope you'll be as happy together as Alice and I have been over these twenty years."

"I know we will be," Sue said, beaming at Jeremy. Then her eyes grew misty. "When my mother died, I felt all alone in the world. Now, not only do I have Jeremy—I have your wonderful, loving family. I don't feel alone anymore."

Jessica was sorry Sue's mother died, but she found Sue's gushiness a little too much to bear. She wondered how Jeremy could stand it.

"You're like the big sister Jessica and Elizabeth never had," Mrs. Wakefield said, smiling at Jessica. "And it's been so nice to have you staying in Steven's room."

"Oh, Steven, I really do appreciate you letting me stay in your room," Sue said.

"I actually like staying in the family room. I like to just flip channels on the TV while I'm falling asleep," Steven said.

"I hope that you and Jeremy will continue coming to stay with us after you're married," Mrs. Wakefield said. "That is, if you don't mind Steven's single bed!"

"We don't mind, do we honey?" Sue said to Jeremy.

I'm going to be sick right now, Jessica thought. *If I sit here one more minute, I'm going to throw up.*

"Oh, I almost forgot, Jess," Elizabeth said as she reached for another waffle. "Lila called and said she wants you to call her back as soon as possible."

Good timing, sis, Jessica thought gratefully. "Excuse me, I have to go return Lila's call," she said, jumping up from the table.

"I guess she's still feeling a little sick from the champagne," Sue said as Jessica ran from the room.

"Guess what!" Lila said excitedly on the phone.

"I'm not in the mood for guessing games," Jessica groaned.

"Robby and I got back together last night at the engagement party," Lila said.

Lila Fowler was Jessica's best friend and the wealthiest girl at Sweet Valley High. Robby Goodman was Jeremy's best friend, and Lila had fallen for Robby the same day Jessica met Jeremy.

"Don't tell me—his rich uncle just died, leaving him his fortune, and now Robby's a millionaire after all," Jessica said sarcastically. When Robby and Lila first met, Robby had pretended to be rich. Then Lila found out that, in fact, Robby was a poor artist, and she'd been furious. It wasn't that she cared so much about the money. What upset her was that he'd lied to her. He'd pretended to be something he wasn't.

"Very funny," Lila said.

"He won the Sweet Valley lottery and the pot was up to ten million dollars," Jessica teased.

"You should really be a stand-up comedienne," Lila said. "Either that or go back to bed and wake up in a better mood."

"Oh, OK," Jessica said. "Tell me how you could have possibly forgiven Robby for what he did."

"Well, he was extremely apologetic and just kept explaining that he only lied to me because he was afraid I might not like him if I found out the truth. He figured that I probably only went out with wealthy guys."

Jessica just let out a skeptical, "Hmmmm."

"What's that supposed to mean?" Lila prodded.

"I'm probably wrong," Jessica said, unable to resist the temptation to stir up a little trouble for her friend. True, she'd encouraged Lila to forgive Robby, but now she was regretting that she'd gotten involved. Jessica was accustomed to being the one with a successful love life and that was how Jessica preferred it. "It just occurred to me that, since Robby's so poor and all, maybe he's only interested in you for your money."

"That's an incredibly mean thing to say," Lila said angrily. "You don't think somebody would like me just for who I am?"

"You know I don't think that. I just don't want Robby to use you," Jessica said.

"He's not using me," Lila said defensively. "And anyway, I've come to realize that money isn't everything."

"Since when?" Jessica asked ruefully.

"Since I realized how lucky I am that my boyfriend is available and not on the verge of marrying someone else," Lila said nastily. "What's going on with lover boy? Are you going to be his mistress after the wedding?"

Jessica knew that Lila was just getting back at her for what she'd said but she was furious.

Mistress? The sound of it sent a chill up and down Jessica's spine. *If Jeremy thinks Jessica Wakefield is mistress material, then he doesn't know Jessica Wakefield.* "I won't play second fiddle to anyone," Jessica declared. "I refuse to be like those women with low self-esteem in that silly 'primal woman' seminar I went to with Elizabeth. I'm going to be numero uno or it's *arrivederci* Jeremy!"

"What are you going to do? Are you going to throw Sue under a truck like you did to Sue's wedding dress? A life sentence might be an obstacle to your relationship with Jeremy," Lila teased.

Lila was referring to the time Jessica purposely threw Sue's wedding dress under a truck. Unfortunately, the whole thing backfired on Jessica when her mother made her pay to repair the damage.

"I don't know what I'm going to do yet, but I'm not going to sit by quietly and just watch things happen around me. And if I were you," Jessica added, "I would be thinking up some way to get back at Robby for pretending to be something he's not. It's time we women take control. Hey, maybe I should start writing those silly books Elizabeth keeps reading," she joked.

Chapter 3

"Isn't this just precious, honey?" Sue asked Jeremy as she pulled out his and hers matching Koala sweatshirts from a box. Sue and Jeremy were in the Wakefields' living room Sunday night, opening their engagement presents from the night before.

"Who are those from?" Elizabeth asked. Elizabeth had assigned herself the job of writing down who had given them each gift.

Jeremy looked through the box and found the card. "They're from my parents in Australia. They say how sorry they are, again, that they can't be at the wedding."

Jeremy looked over at Jessica, who refused to return his gaze. *He'll realize that I'm not going to play second fiddle to anybody.* Ever since Jessica's phone conversation with Lila that morning, she couldn't get the word "mistress" out of her head. What was Jeremy planning to do anyway? If he cared for Jessica the way he said he did, how could he go through with the wedding? *Was* he thinking Jessica would be his mistress?

"I wish your parents could be here for the wedding, honey," Sue said.

"What are they doing in Australia?" Steven asked as he ate a piece of peach cobbler, Elizabeth's contribution to the new "cook off" they'd started that morning.

"They're on a world tour for a year," Jeremy said, still looking at Jessica. "For as long as I can remember, Dad was always planning to travel around the world as soon as he retired. They wanted to come for the wedding, but I insisted that they just enjoy their trip. We'll celebrate with them when they come back."

"Look at these gorgeous satin sheets from the Fowlers, honey," Sue said to Jeremy. "I adore satin."

Satin sheets? Jessica thought. The idea of them together on those pink satin sheets gave Jessica a sick feeling.

"Isn't that a great serving platter?" Mrs. Wakefield exclaimed as Sue pulled a big silver tray from a box.

"It is nice," Sue said as she turned it over to read the back. "Well, actually," she said, scrunching up her face, "it's not sterling silver. It's only pewter."

"I don't think we'll really need sterling silver when we're hiking around the rainforests," Jeremy said, smiling at Sue. "Pewter's probably better for our lifestyle."

"I guess you're right, honey," Sue said, putting the tray back in its box.

Jessica had had enough. She got up to clear the cobbler plates and realized that Jeremy had followed her into the kitchen.

"Hey, beautiful," Jeremy said, coming up behind Jessica.

As much as she wanted Jeremy to know she was mad at him, she couldn't help breaking into an enormous smile. She turned around to face him and allowed him to put his arms around her.

"You know, Sue or my parents could walk in at any minute," Jessica said, wishing that Sue *would* walk in on them together.

"I don't care," Jeremy said. "I was going crazy in there. It's torture being in the same room and not being able to put my arms around you."

"I know what you mean. We can't keep going on like this though—sneaking around behind everyone's back," Jessica said, although the truth was that she loved the idea of sharing a fleeting moment with Jeremy while his fiancée sat unknowingly in the next room.

"That's what I wanted to talk to you about,"

Jeremy said as he moved a strand of Jessica's hair out of her face.

Jessica held her breath and crossed her fingers in anticipation of him saying what she wanted to hear.

"I'm taking Sue out to a movie tonight," Jeremy started, causing Jessica to pull away from him. "Wait a minute. I'm taking her out so that I can see you later."

"What do you mean?" Jessica asked, making a skeptical face. "How will your seeing Sue help me and you be together?"

"When I drop Sue back off at your house, I'll blow my horn, drive down the street, and wait at the end of the block. You'll sneak out of the house and meet me in my car," Jeremy said.

"And then what?" Jessica asked.

"Then we'll go where we can be alone somewhere," Jeremy said.

I would go to the end of the world with you, Jessica wanted to blurt out. Jessica was thrilled that finally, they would have a chance to be alone together for more than just a few minutes.

"What do you think? The low-cut T-shirt or the body suit?" Jessica asked Elizabeth.

"I think you should wear one of Dad's old overcoats and put a nun's wimple on your head," Elizabeth said wryly.

38

"Very funny," Jessica retorted.

Jessica was standing in front of the full-length mirror in her bedroom, trying on a dozen different outfits for her date with Jeremy. Elizabeth was sitting on Jessica's bed, reading her book about love addiction.

"OK, listen to this," Elizabeth said, clearing her throat. "'Women who are love-addicted are unable to differentiate between men who are good for them and men who are bad for them. They become so overtaken by their desire for a man that they overlook his negatives.'"

"I'm really not in the mood for this right now," Jessica said as she tried on a tight miniskirt. "All I want to think about is my date."

"Take that tacky skirt off," Elizabeth commanded. "This part totally speaks to your situation, so just be quiet and listen."

Jessica took another look at herself in the miniskirt, and deciding that Elizabeth was right—it was a little tacky—took it off. She searched frantically for something else while Elizabeth read out loud.

"'For example,'" Elizabeth continued, "'some women will overlook the fact that a man is involved with someone else. Her need for this man is so overwhelming that she refuses to see the reality of the situation. It's like an alcoholic who needs another drink even if he knows that drink will ruin his life. A woman will continue her involvement with an unavailable man even though she knows that he will never be hers.'"

"I have a huge favor to ask you, Lizzie," Jessica said, using a very sweet, innocent voice.

"Are you even listening to what I'm reading?" Elizabeth asked, annoyed.

"Yes, it's fascinating," Jessica said, rolling her eyes. "But what I really need is for you to let me borrow your new tight designer jeans."

"Over my dead body," Elizabeth said. "I refuse to support you in this unhealthy relationship in any way."

"Please," Jessica begged. "What if I promise to read one of your stupid self-help books?"

"No way," Elizabeth said. "I refuse to be party to your deception. And stop calling my books stupid." Elizabeth had a plan to keep her twin from leaving the house that night, but she had to keep up the front of being concerned about it.

"It's not like you're Miss Perfect yourself," Jessica said. "It seems to me that you were practicing a little deception yourself in London if I remember correctly. Did you write a letter to Todd telling him about Luke? I don't think so."

"Can we please not talk about that?" Elizabeth, feeling queazy, looked down at her book.

"Well, I just think you should worry about your own life before you go around making judgments about other people's," Jessica said.

"I know that what I did in London was wrong, and that's why I'm reading these books," Elizabeth said. "I'm slowly rediscovering myself and learning why I let myself lose control so it doesn't happen again. And that's why I think you should read this book about love addiction so you don't lose control with Jeremy."

"It's too late to change what you've already done, and just because you're reading some silly books doesn't take away the fact that you deceived Todd," Jessica said.

She's right, Elizabeth thought to herself. *I'm just as deceitful as Jessica.* Elizabeth knew she should tell Todd about Luke when he got back from his grandmother's but she couldn't stand the idea of hurting him, and more importantly, she was scared to death that he would break up with her. He'd never understand how she could have gotten so involved with somebody else when everything had been so good between them before she left. It was totally out of character for her to have done something like falling in love with another guy. Especially with a psycho who thought he was a werewolf. She still didn't know why she had allowed herself to lose control like that.

Elizabeth was almost always sure of what to do in most situations. Especially when it was a question of right and wrong. This time, however, she

41

wasn't sure. She hated feeling so uncertain about what to do. Also, she hated to think that she was on the same level as Jessica in terms of deception. *How can I judge Jeremy and Jessica if I'm guilty of the same thing?*

"It's him!" Jessica said out loud to herself in her bedroom later that evening when she heard Jeremy's horn. She spritzed herself with perfume and checked her outfit in the mirror for the twentieth time. She had finally decided on black jeans and a purple tank top. She put the slightest bit of lipstick and blush on, then practiced her smile in the mirror. She figured that Jeremy would prefer the "natural look" since he was such an outdoorsman. He was probably the kind of guy that didn't like girls to wear a lot of makeup.

This is it, she thought to herself. *I'm going to tell him tonight that he has to decide once and for all between me or Sue. I have to let him know that I won't share him with another woman.*

But when Jessica tried to open her bedroom door, it was locked. She rushed to the bathroom door that connected hers to Elizabeth's bedroom and it was locked, too. *Elizabeth did this! How dare she try to sabotage my date with Jeremy*, Jessica thought, furious with her twin. She looked around her room for something to break the lock with, and finding a bobbypin, she stuck it in the keyhole. After what seemed like an eternity, Jessica finally heard the sound of the lock turn over and she flung open the door.

Jessica flew down the stairs and ran smack into Sue. "Where are you off to in such a hurry?" Sue asked.

Jessica, struck speechless, just stared at her blankly.

"Late date with Bruce?" Sue asked smiling.

"Yes!" Jessica said, happy that Sue had bailed her out. "I'm going out for ice cream with Bruce, and he hates it when I'm late," Jessica lied.

"Well, you certainly do look adorable," Sue said. "I'm sure Bruce will think so, too."

"Thanks," Jessica said as she flew out the door, thinking about how much she was starting to hate the word "adorable."

Jessica ran down the street as fast as she could, determined that everything would work out with Jeremy the way she hoped it would. *If you want something so much, it has to come true*, Jessica thought as she saw Jeremy's car waiting on the corner. She had never wanted anything as much as she wanted Jeremy.

"Finally," Jeremy said as he pulled Jessica toward him in the car. "Tonight we can make a clean getaway."

"Jeremy, we can't always be running away like

43

this," Jessica said, even though she had to admit that she found their secretiveness extremely romantic.

"I know," Jeremy said. "That's what I want to talk to you about."

Elizabeth was eating a big piece of chocolate mousse cake left over from the engagement party while she sat at the kitchen table reading her love addiction book. She was hoping her book would give her some answers about how to handle Jessica's situation with Jeremy and her own situation with Todd.

She'd known Jessica would figure out how to get out of her room. She just hadn't known she'd be able to do it so quickly.

Next time, I'll have to move heavy furniture in front of her door.

"Hey, that looks good. Mind if I join you?" Sue asked as she came into the kitchen.

"I'd love you to finish it," Elizabeth said between bites, wondering how she was supposed to look Sue in the eye, knowing what she knew. "I'm afraid if I sit here alone in the same room with it, I'm going to devour the whole thing."

Act normal, she told herself, helping herself to a second piece of cake. She thought the chocolate would help calm her nerves, which were completely out of whack at that moment. Jessica was totally out of control, and worse than that, Todd was coming back to Sweet Valley the next day, and she still hadn't decided what she was going to do.

"I know what you mean," Sue said as she cut herself a big piece. "When it comes to chocolate, I have absolutely no willpower."

"Me neither," Elizabeth agreed. "I guess you could say I'm a chocolate addict."

"I just saw your sister running out of the house on her way to her date," Sue said.

"Her date?" Elizabeth asked, her eyes wide. *Don't tell me Sue knows*, Elizabeth thought, panicked.

"Yeah, she had a date with Bruce Patman," Sue said cheerfully. "She seemed really excited. They must be serious."

"Umm . . ."

"I was excited like that when Jeremy and I first started seeing each other," Sue continued. "It was like a fairy tale. I used to change my outfit a million different times whenever we were about to go on a date. When I realized that Jeremy felt the same way about me, I thought I was living a dream. I had never been so happy in all my life. Meeting Jeremy was the best thing that ever happened to me."

"That's so romantic," said Elizabeth, angrier than ever at her twin. Sue looked so happy and innocent as she ate her piece of cake. *She has no clue that she's being betrayed right under her nose.*

"Isn't your beau supposed to be back here soon?" Sue asked eagerly. "I can't wait to meet him. You must be getting excited to see him again."

Elizabeth wished she *did* feel excited about seeing Todd but instead she was dreading his return. "To tell you the truth, I'm afraid to see him again because of all that stuff I told you about Luke." Elizabeth had shared the grisly story with Sue one day at the beach. "I still haven't decided whether or not to tell him about it."

"When it comes to love," Sue said, "I really believe in honesty. Just the smallest lie can start a disease that can destroy your relationship over time. If you really love Todd and want to be with him then you have to tell him the truth."

"Sometimes I don't know if I do or not," Elizabeth said. "I just don't know if I'll ever be able to trust anyone ever again." Elizabeth wanted to say, *and you shouldn't trust Jeremy*, but she kept her mouth shut.

"You feel like that now because Luke hurt you, but you can't go through life like that," Sue said. "Life is about taking risks and falling in love is definitely a risk. Sure, there's always a chance that your heart might get broken but you know what they say, "'Tis better to have loved and lost than never to have loved at all.'"

"Yes, well," Elizabeth started, wondering if Sue would be so magnanimous when it came to losing Jeremy, "there's a letter on the table in the front hallway for you." She was desperate to change the subject. "It's been there since yesterday. I'm sorry nobody told you it was there."

"That's OK," Sue said, looking down at her cake. "I actually knew it was there. I just haven't gotten around to opening it yet."

Maybe Sue's right. Maybe I should tell Todd everything, Elizabeth thought, tuning Sue out. *If he really loves me, he'll forgive me.*

"This is a great restaurant," Robby said as he looked over the menu at La Maison Blanche, one of the fanciest restaurants in Sweet Valley. "I wish I was the one treating you tonight. It's the least I could do to make everything up to you."

"Don't be silly," Lila said as she ran a hand through her straight brown hair and smiled at the gorgeous, dark-haired Adonis sitting across the table. "It doesn't matter who's inviting who. What matters is that we're together again."

"You're right," Robby said as he smothered a hot roll with butter. "But some night soon you'll have to let me cook for you. I'm a whiz in the kitchen."

"It's a deal," Lila said. Even though Lila knew

that Jessica probably wouldn't approve of her taking Robby out to a fancy restaurant, she didn't care. She was just so happy to be back together with Robby, and she wanted them to have a romantic evening together. Lila loved expensive restaurants, so why should they have to go to the Dairi Burger or a pizza parlor when she could afford to take them somewhere special?

"I'll have the house salad," Robby said to the waiter when he came to take their order.

That's really sweet, Lila thought to herself. *He's just getting a salad because he doesn't want to take advantage of my money.* Lila couldn't wait to tell Jessica that she had been all wrong about Robby being interested only in her money.

"And then I'll have the filet mignon," Robby added.

Lila looked down at the menu. Filet mignon was the most expensive item on the menu. Twenty dollars for a piece of meat! *Maybe he didn't realize how much it costs*, Lila reasoned, trying to reassure herself. *And it's not as if I can't afford it. Besides, I don't want him to starve himself.*

She decided just to let it go and not make a big deal about it. After all, she was in this incredibly romantic atmosphere with a guy she was crazy about. She was wearing her new sleeveless red velvet dress and pearls, and she didn't want anything to spoil the evening. Especially not the nagging voice of Jessica that she kept hearing in her head.

"So, have you had much success selling your paintings?" Lila asked Robby after she ordered the fresh salmon.

"No, I haven't," Robby said.

"Well, my parents know a lot of people in the gallery world. I could introduce you to some people who could help you," Lila offered.

"To tell you the truth, I'm not really interested in selling my work," Robby said. He took a sip of the mineral water the waiter poured into his glass.

"You're not interested in selling your paintings?"

"That's right. I feel like my art would somehow lose its integrity if I started painting with the idea of pleasing a potential buyer," Robby said before plunging into his salad with zeal.

"But don't you want to share your work with other people?" Lila asked. "It seems sad to deprive the world of your talent."

"I don't really see it that way," Robby said.

So you're just going to stay penniless your whole life? Lila thought. *That seems like a pretty bad idea considering your expensive taste.*

Chapter 4

"Look! A shooting star!" Jessica said to Jeremy as they sat in his car with the roof down, looking out at the billions of stars above them. They had driven up the coast to Miller's Point. Jessica had been breathless the whole ride up as her hair blew in the breeze and she felt the chill press against her face. She had to keep pinching herself to make sure she wasn't just dreaming. She really *was* with the man she loved and they were alone together at last. Even though she was still mad and hurt that he hadn't told Sue about them yet, she was happy just to be with him.

"When I see all these stars, it helps me keep life in perspective," Jeremy said as Jessica cradled her head on his shoulder. "It helps me realize what's important in life."

"How do you mean?" Jessica asked as she felt Jeremy's arms around her. She had never felt as safe and protected as she felt at that moment.

"I just see how small our lives are compared to the rest of the universe. We just have these little lives that don't last very long if you compare them to the lives of stars or trees," Jeremy said as he stroked Jessica's hair.

"I see what you mean," Jessica said. If Jeremy had said that he believed in UFOs, she probably would have said the same thing. She would have agreed with anything he said as long as she could stay there in his arms, looking up at the sky.

"We only live once, and that's why we have to do exactly what we want with our lives," Jeremy said.

"And marrying Sue is what you want to do with your life?" Jessica asked, looking up at him.

"I thought that's what I wanted," Jeremy said, sighing heavily. "But now, everything's different. When I first met Sue, she seemed so lonely and lost. She came to me to see about doing an internship at Project Nature. I told her we didn't need anybody else, but she looked like she was going to burst into tears."

"So, you gave her the internship," Jessica said. What she really wanted to say was, *You should have just let her cry. She's a big girl. She would have been just fine.*

"I just couldn't say no," Jeremy said. "She

seemed so desperate for the job. Also, she seemed so alone in the world. Her mother was very ill and her stepfather was always away on business. She was so in need of affection and purpose that I couldn't turn my back on her."

"So you started working together," Jessica said.

"Right," Jeremy said. "We spent practically every moment together. She became just as passionate about saving the rain forests as I was. We were really compatible and we had this common bond."

"And you fell in love?" Jessica asked, trying to sound simply curious and nonchalant.

"She did and I thought I did too, but I never really did," Jeremy admitted.

Jessica had been holding her breath until he said exactly what she wanted to hear.

"I care about her, but it's not the same as—" Jeremy said, then stopped himself.

"Not the same as what?" Jessica pressed.

"It's not the same as when I was seventeen and hopelessly in love with a girl named Justine," Jeremy said. "I felt like I didn't want to live if I couldn't be with her. Every time I saw her my heart stopped. She was the first thing I thought of when I woke up in the morning and the last thing I thought of before I went to sleep."

"What happened to Justine? " Jessica asked, hoping he'd say she was in a convent.

"It didn't work out. We both went off to separate colleges," Jeremy said. "I heard she got married and had a kid. I think she lives in Alaska now. Anyway, the point is that I never felt that way about Sue. I just thought that was because I'd gotten older. I figured it was just crazy teenage love. I thought I'd never feel that way again but that maybe I could learn to feel something close to that with Sue. So when she asked me to marry her, I thought, why not?"

"*She* asked *you*?" Jessica asked, incredulous.

"Yeah," Jeremy said. "It seemed like a good idea at the time. We made a good team. She was so attached to me and had such a need to have some security in her life. And I had become attached to her, too. I just resigned myself to the fact that I would never feel that kind of crazy love again until—"

"Until what?" Jessica asked urgently.

"Until I met you," Jeremy said, looking into Jessica's eyes. "Jessica, I'm in love with you. I've known it since the first day we met. I just couldn't admit it to myself. I see now that there's no way I can marry Sue. I would be living a lie."

Jessica couldn't believe what she was hearing. She thought she was going to burst into tears out of sheer happiness. Her dream had come true. He was in love with her, and he was calling off the wedding. "What will you tell Sue?" Jessica asked.

"I'm just going to tell her the truth," Jeremy said with an extremely serious tone in his voice. "I'll tell her that I'll always be there for her as a friend. I'll try to make her see that it would be more unfair to her in the long run if I went through with the wedding."

"When are you going to tell her?" Jessica asked, trying not to sound too eager.

"I have to go meet with some fund-raisers for the rain forest preservation effort all day tomorrow, so I'll have to wait and tell her tomorrow afternoon," Jeremy said.

"Of course I'm sorry for Sue," Jessica lied. "But I must admit that you've made me happier than I've ever been in my entire life."

Jeremy grabbed Jessica and kissed her more passionately than Jessica had ever been kissed before.

Elizabeth was on her way to her room when she thought she heard the sound of crying coming from Sue's room. She knocked on the door and let herself in. *She knows!* Elizabeth thought as she saw Sue leaning over with her hands covering her face. When Sue looked up, her eyes were bloodshot and her eyelids were all puffy.

"Sue, what is it?" Elizabeth asked tentatively, knowing exactly what it was. "Do you want to talk?"

"Everything's fine," Sue said, obviously lying. "I

guess I'm just a little nervous about the wedding and everything."

"Sue, tell me the truth," Elizabeth pressed gently. It would be better for everyone if this thing between Jessica and Jeremy were finally out in the open. "Isn't there something you want to tell me about?"

"You're right," Sue said sadly. "There is something I need to talk to you about, but I want you to keep it a secret. Especially from your parents."

That's too unbelievably kind. She doesn't want Mom and Dad to know about Jeremy and Jessica because she doesn't want to get Jessica in trouble. This girl is a saint. "I promise not to say anything to anybody," Elizabeth said. "And actually, I might already know more than you might think."

Sue shook her head. "No, there's no way you could know about this."

Elizabeth felt terribly guilty. *She doesn't think I could know about Jeremy and Jessica because she probably assumes I would have told her. She trusts me.* "Well, why don't you just tell me what it is that's on your mind."

Sue's lip started to quiver and all the color seemed to drain from her face. She lowered her voice to a grave whisper and held up the letter Elizabeth had told her about earlier. "It's about this."

"What is it? Bad news about someone in your family?" Elizabeth asked.

"Bad news about me," Sue said.

"Oh, no," Elizabeth said. "Is it something about the wedding?" *Did Jeremy send her a letter, breaking off the wedding? What a coward! Or maybe Jessica!*

Sue drew in a big breath and smoothed out the pink silk robe and nightgown she was wearing. "Elizabeth, I'm very sick."

"What do you mean? Do you have the flu or something like that?" Elizabeth asked.

"I wish that's all it was," Sue said sadly. "I'm afraid it's more serious than that. My mother died of a very rare blood disease that the doctors knew almost nothing about. All they knew was that it was genetic and that there was no cure for it."

"I'm so sorry. That must have been so painful for you."

"It was horrible," Sue said then paused. "But the bad news is that I have the same disease. I took a series of tests right before I came to California, and I just got back the results. If the doctors are right, I only have two or three years to live."

Elizabeth was trying to take in everything that Sue was telling her. How could this be? This beautiful, young woman who was planning to get married and travel around the world was dying? It couldn't be true.

"Sue, are you sure? Maybe they got the test results mixed up, or . . ."

Sue smiled. "I went through that denial myself, Elizabeth, but I'm afraid there's no doubt. I have the same disease my mother had, and it's going to kill me the same way it killed her."

Elizabeth, not knowing what to say, leaned over and hugged Sue. The two sat like that in silence while they both wept softly. Finally, Elizabeth spoke, tears streaming down her face. "I just don't know what to say. It's so unfair. Have you told Jeremy?"

"I haven't told him yet." Sue wiped a tear from her cheek and slicked back her short brown hair with the palm of her hand. "I'm going to tell him tomorrow. And I'm going to tell him that the wedding's off."

"What do you mean?" Elizabeth said, afraid again that Sue knew about Jessica and Jeremy.

"I just can't do that to Jeremy," Sue said. "I can't marry him knowing that I'll only be alive for a short while. He's still young and healthy and he needs a wife who is as full of life as he is. It's an unfair burden to place on him when he's in the midst of his career taking off. He has too many things he needs to do. It would hurt me terribly to keep him from his dreams."

"But I'm sure Jeremy would rather spend as much time as possible with you until—" Elizabeth couldn't bear to finish the sentence. "Besides, who knows what could happen in the next couple of years. You could have a miraculous recovery or they could discover a cure. There are major medical breakthroughs all the time."

"I wish everything you're saying were true," Sue said, taking Elizabeth's hand in her own. "I appreciate you being so hopeful but I have to be realistic. This is my decision and I'm going to have to stick with it."

"I just wish you'd reconsider," Elizabeth pleaded. She felt desperate about Sue's marrying Jeremy. She believed that if Sue could be happy and realize her dream of marrying Jeremy, maybe somehow she wouldn't be sick anymore. *This should keep Jessica away from Jeremy now. There's no way even Jessica would continue to deceive a dying woman.*

Jessica floated up the stairs to her room after her magical date with Jeremy. *After tomorrow, Jeremy will be all mine*, she thought dreamily. *We won't have to sneak around anymore. We can tell the whole world that we're in love. I knew from that very first moment I laid eyes on him that we were meant to be together and now we will be. I'm truly the luckiest girl in the world.*

She opened the door to her room and found Elizabeth sitting on her bed. "Liz," Jessica said, "I'm happier than I've been in my whole life. You won't believe what Jeremy just told me."

"We have to talk," Elizabeth said sternly.

"I know," Jessica said. "I want to tell you all

59

about what just happened with Jeremy." She looked at herself in the mirror to see how she looked when she was just with Jeremy. She liked what she saw. Her smile seemed brighter and broader than ever.

Over her shoulder in the mirror, Jessica caught Elizabeth's expression. She had that judgmental look that seemed to be permanently plastered on her face lately. "Are you going to give me a ticket for breaking out of jail and being out too late?" Jessica said, spinning around from the mirror. "Isn't that what you Date Police do? I'm guilty. Arrest me." Jessica put her hands up in the air, pretending to be a captured criminal. "Which reminds me. Locking me in here was a rotten thing to do, not to mention a fire hazard. You're lucky I'm in such a wonderful mood right now. Otherwise, you'd really be in for it."

"Jess," Elizabeth said in a serious voice. "Sit down right now."

Jessica walked over to her bed and pushed Elizabeth to the side, making room for herself to crawl in under the covers.

"OK, what's so incredibly important that you can't wait until the morning to tell me?" Jessica asked, propping herself up on her pillows.

Elizabeth looked down at the floor then back at Jessica. "It's about Sue," Elizabeth said. "You have to stop this thing with Jeremy immediately."

"I told you I don't want any lectures tonight," Jessica said, losing her patience. "My love life is my business. I know everything you're going to say, and frankly, I don't want to hear it."

"It's not just your business," Elizabeth said. "You're deceiving a dying woman."

"Oh, please." Jessica was totally irritated. "You've really gone overboard now, Liz. Those books you've been reading have done something to your brain. People get upset over heartbreak but they don't die over it. Maybe Romeo and Juliet— but they're an exception."

"Listen to me!" Elizabeth commanded urgently. "Sue is dying. She has an incurable, rare blood disease. She has about three years to live."

"Is this some kind of bad joke?" Jessica asked, although she knew it was unlike Elizabeth to make up stories like that. "If this is your new way of getting me to stop seeing Jeremy, I think you've gone a little too far."

"Jessica, it's true. It's the same disease her mother died of. She just got the results back from some tests she took before she came here. She told me tonight."

Jessica saw that Elizabeth's eyes were full of tears. At that moment, she knew that Elizabeth wasn't playing a joke. *She's telling the truth! How can this be happening? I've made Sue sick. I wanted Jeremy so badly that I somehow willed Sue*

61

out of the picture. I even said to Elizabeth that I wished she would just disappear. But I didn't mean I wanted her to die! Jessica had thought in the past that she had psychic powers. Now she believed that all her bad thoughts about Sue were somehow responsible for Sue's being sick. She felt as if she'd been punched in the stomach.

Tears rolled down Jessica's face. "I feel worse than I've ever felt in my life. And to think that just a few moments ago I felt happier than I've ever felt in my life. I'm a terrible person. This is all my fault."

"It's not your fault," Elizabeth consoled. "You don't have anything to do with Sue being sick. But obviously, you can't keep seeing Jeremy. I'm sure you see why that has to end right away."

Jeremy. Jessica closed her eyes and saw his face. She could still smell his cologne and feel his hands stroking her hair. How could she give up the only man she'd ever love? How could she *not* give him up knowing what she knew about Sue? Suddenly, unbidden, an idea popped into her head. At first, she thought it was crazy but the more she thought about it, the more it made sense.

"What if Sue's lying?" Jessica asked.

"What?" Elizabeth gasped.

"What if Sue's only pretending to be sick because she doesn't want to lose Jeremy?" Jessica was sitting up excitedly on her bed and her eyes widened. "What if she knows about me and Jeremy and is afraid he's about to call off the wedding? Maybe this is the only way she can think of to keep him!"

"You really are sick, Jessica Wakefield," Elizabeth said in utter disgust. Jessica saw that Elizabeth's entire body was shaking. She'd never seen her sister so angry. "You're about the most evil, unfeeling, selfish person in the world. I can't believe my own sister is capable of saying such horrid things about somebody who's dying. I can't even believe you're my sister, let alone my twin."

"But just think about it—" Jessica started.

"No, you think about this," Elizabeth said sternly as she stood up. "For your information, Ms. Sherlock Holmes, Sue is calling off the wedding."

"What do you mean?" Jessica asked.

"She is so unselfish—unlike other people—that she doesn't want to put Jeremy through the pain of losing his wife. So, in order to protect her poor, deceitful, two-timing fiance, she's going to forfeit the one thing in life that could give her a little pleasure before she dies! I guess that kind of blows that ugly, monstrous theory of yours out of the water!" Elizabeth marched out of the room and slammed the door behind her.

She's calling off the wedding? Jessica didn't know what she felt. That disproved her theory that Sue was making up the story of her sickness in order to keep Jeremy. What would all of this mean for her and Jeremy? She wasn't sure, but she was afraid it wouldn't be good.

Chapter 5

Elizabeth woke up the next morning and immediately wanted to go back to sleep. *Sue is dying. It's just all so sad and tragic and there's nothing I can do about it.* Elizabeth didn't know if she'd be able to forgive Jessica for saying those terrible things about poor Sue. She pulled the covers over her head and closed her eyes, but she couldn't fall asleep again.

As if she didn't have enough to worry about already, today was Monday, the day Todd was coming back from his grandmother's. She still hadn't decided whether or not she was going to tell him the truth about what happened in London. After all the mess with Jeremy and Jessica, she didn't want to be guilty of deceiving someone herself.

But how could she hurt Todd like that? Not

only did she have a fling with somebody, but she had shown such poor judgment. How could she explain to Todd that she'd fallen for a crazy English guy who dressed up like a werewolf and killed his victims by tearing out their throats? When the truth had finally come out, all she'd wanted was to see Todd again. She'd realized more than ever just how kind and trustworthy Todd was. *How could I deceive someone like Todd? Now that I realize how special he is, it might be too late! Why does love have to be so hard? Sue loves Jeremy but he loves Jessica, who loves him. And I love Todd and he loves me, but I thought I loved Luke and, because of that, Todd will probably stop loving me!*

Elizabeth felt overwhelmed and paralyzed by the weight of everyone's problems, including her own. Everything and everyone seemed doomed. *Maybe I could say I'm sick and just stay in bed all day*, Elizabeth thought. *There's no way I can face Jessica, Jeremy, Sue, and especially Todd today. If Todd calls, I'll tell him I'm too sick to see him.*

"Elizabeth!" Mrs. Wakefield yelled from the bottom of the stairs. Elizabeth braced herself for what she was going to say.

"Todd's here to see you!" Elizabeth pulled the covers over her head, then threw them off, knowing there was no way to postpone misery.

✧   ✧   ✧

"I've decided to take your advice about Robby," Lila said to Jessica between bites of her cheeseburger. The two girls were having lunch at the Dairi Burger.

Jessica had agreed to meet Lila after she'd given up her idea of trying to find Jeremy that morning. She was desperate to talk to him about Sue's illness and to find out what that would mean for them. She knew he'd said something about meeting with fund-raisers, but still, she had driven all over Sweet Valley in search of his white rented car. She would just have to wait until later that afternoon even though it was making her crazy.

"What advice?" Jessica asked before sucking loudly on her straw. She was so nervous about Jeremy that she had managed to drink an entire chocolate milkshake without even realizing it.

"Your advice about getting back at him for making me think he was so wealthy," Lila said, obviously annoyed that her friend wasn't paying attention.

"Oh, that," Jessica said, jumping out of her thoughts about Jeremy for the moment. "So, what are you going to do?"

"I'm going to make him think that he's not the only one who's poor." Lila smiled and popped one of Jessica's french fries into her mouth.

"What do you mean?" Jessica asked.

"Well, I'm going to see if he's still interested in me even if I'm not rich."

"I've been wanting to talk to you about that," Jessica said. "I was really out of line when I said that to you about him only being interested in your money. I'm sure he really likes you for you. It was a dumb thing for me to say." Jessica surprised herself by being so nice to Lila. She figured it was a result of still feeling a little guilty about Sue, even if she had her doubts about whether or not she was really sick.

"I'm not so sure," Lila said as her smile gave way to a worried expression. Lila explained the events of the night before at La Maison Blanche with Robby.

"Hmmmm," Jessica uttered, taking in the information. "He certainly has expensive tastes for a starving artist."

"I know. And I won't feel comfortable until I'm certain that he's not with me just because I can foot the bill!"

Elizabeth's heart was racing as she walked down the stairs. While she was getting dressed, she'd decided to take Sue's advice and tell Todd the truth. When she saw Todd standing in the foyer, his back turned to her, she felt her knees go weak. Just the sight of his shoulders made her want to wrap her arms around him. *Stay in control*, she told herself. *Don't lose your cool just because he's so gorgeous.*

Todd turned around when he heard Elizabeth coming down the stairs and his face broke into an enormous smile. "I can't believe I'm really seeing you," Todd said as he held out his arms. "It seems like it's been forever."

Despite Elizabeth's resolve to stay in control, she ran into Todd's arms and kissed him on the lips. "You have no idea how glad I am to see you," Elizabeth said as she rested her head against his chest. *And I just hope you're still going to be glad to see me after I tell you what I have to tell you.*

"Let's get out of here and hit the beach," Todd said. "We have a lot to talk about."

In the car, Todd talked on about all the things he did while he was staying at his grandmother's house. He practiced basketball every day and read every book on his summer reading list. He even went to a nursing home a couple of times a week and read out loud to the senior citizens.

Elizabeth was unusually quiet but Todd didn't seem to notice since he was so busy chatting away. He was in such a good mood and was acting like everything was just the same as before he left that she was dreading bursting his bubble.

"Todd," Elizabeth said as she turned to face him on the beach. "There's something I need to talk to you about."

They plopped down on the sand and looked out at the ocean. Todd brushed Elizabeth's hair from her face and kissed her quickly on the lips. "It's really great to see you, Elizabeth. Every time I got a postcard from England, my heart jumped for joy. It sounded like you had a great time. You have no idea how much I missed you."

"I know. I missed you too," Elizabeth said, feeling guiltier than ever. "But there's something I have to tell you that I didn't write about in my postcards." *And after I tell you, you'll probably never want to see me again*, she thought.

"Actually," Todd interrupted. "There's something I have to tell you first." Todd drew in a deep breath, looked up, and then turned to look at Elizabeth with a super-serious expression on his face. "I met someone this summer."

"What do you mean?" Elizabeth was so nervous about making her confession that she wasn't sure she'd understood him.

Todd cleared his throat. "There was this girl who lived next door to my grandmother, and we spent a lot of time together. It didn't come close to what you and I have together but still I thought you should know about it. It ended really badly. She was pretending to be something she wasn't the whole time. I guess I liked her because she reminded me of you. She would tell me how much she liked to read all these great books, but when I

70

asked her about them, it turned out she hadn't really read them. When it was over, I realized that all I'd wanted was to be with you. I guess I missed you so much that I was looking for a temporary substitute. I'm really sorry, Elizabeth. It was a terrible mistake and when it was over, all I could think about was coming back to Sweet Valley and seeing you."

Elizabeth was stunned. *I was right,* she thought. *You can't trust anybody!* She felt a lump in her throat and she bit her lip so she wouldn't start crying. "How could you? I trusted you. I thought about you the whole time I was in London."

"I'm so sorry." Todd looked like he was about to cry. "I thought about you the whole time, too. It really was nothing. I promise. You're the only one I care about. I know that more than ever now."

"What's her name?" Elizabeth asked curtly. She stared at the water in front of her, refusing to look at Todd.

"It doesn't matter now. It's over," Todd said.

"I don't care if it matters or not. I want to know." Elizabeth had never spoken to Todd in such a mean and cold voice as she did at that moment.

"Liz, please try to calm down and see how silly the whole thing is," Todd said, standing up and putting his arms around her.

Elizabeth pulled away from him. "I'll tell you what's silly. You and I being together is silly." Elizabeth ran down the beach and away from Todd without looking back.

Jessica was sitting in the kitchen that afternoon, reading her new *Ingenue* magazine and drinking a diet pop when she heard Jeremy's car pull into the driveway. She leapt up from the table, knocking her drink on the floor. She was on her way to the front door when she saw Sue open it and throw her arms around Jeremy. She peered out from the kitchen and heard him tell Sue that he needed to talk to her about something important.

This is the moment I've been waiting for! He's going to tell Sue everything, and I'll finally have him all to myself, Jessica thought gleefully. She remembered Sue's illness and tried to push the guilty pang away.

Jeremy and Sue went into Mr. Wakefield's study and when the door closed, Jessica pressed her ear against it. Their conversation did concern her, after all.

"Sue, there's something I need to tell you, although I honestly wish I didn't have to," Jeremy started.

"Wait," Sue interrupted. "I have something really important I need to tell you first."

"Can't it wait?" Jeremy asked.

"No, it can't," Sue said, and slowly and methodically told Jeremy all about her terminal disease. "And I'm calling off the wedding," Sue said when she was finished.

"What do you mean?" Jeremy asked.

"I can't put you through the agony of marrying me then losing me," Sue said. "I don't want you to have to live through all the unpleasantness of me being sick. I love you too much to hurt you like that."

"I won't hear of it," Jeremy said, to Jessica's horror. "I'm staying with you until the end. 'Til death do us part. I'm not going to leave you when you need me more than ever. You have to believe that you'll get better. Sometimes miracles *do* happen."

"I do believe in miracles," Sue said. "It was a miracle that I met you."

After that, there was another long silence and Jessica had the sickening feeling that they were either hugging or kissing. She felt like she'd just been slapped in the face. All of her dreams had just gone up in smoke. Jeremy was going through with the wedding even though he was in love with her. He was such a kind and responsible person that he was willing to sacrifice his own happiness for a dying woman.

Jessica tiptoed back to the kitchen and watched while they walked out of the study hand in hand. Sue looked like a tragic heroine from a movie and Jeremy looked like her somber hero—willing to do anything for the damsel in distress.

Chapter 6

"That was a great movie," Robby said to Lila on their way out of the Sweet Valley Cinema that Monday night. He pulled Lila close to him on the street and gave her a kiss on the lips.

"What was that for?" Lila asked.

"That was because you've been so generous and understanding with me," Robby said. "I really appreciate you buying my movie ticket tonight. I thought I had more cash in my wallet. I'll make it up to you soon."

"Don't worry about it," Lila said, then looked down at the ground. "Robby, there's something I need to talk to you about."

"Sure," Robby said, leading her by the hand to a nearby bench on the street. "Is something wrong?"

"Well, it depends on how you react to what I'm about to tell you," Lila said, trying to look serious and sad. "It's about money."

"Look, I'm so sorry about deceiving you like that," Robby said. "You have no idea how grateful I am to you that you forgave me. I see that money really isn't important to you. I know you like me just for me."

Lila and Robby sat close together on the bench under the stars as the couples walked by on their way out of the movie theater. Lila looked at Robby with his dark good looks set off by his white oxford-cloth shirt, and she wondered for a split second if she should really go through with her plan. *He did apologize*, Lila reminded herself. *But still, I need to teach him a lesson*. Lila pulled her straight brown hair out of her ponytail holder and let it hang loosely around her shoulders.

"Robby, I'm not wealthy," Lila blurted out. "In fact, I'm probably even poorer than you are."

"What are you talking about? What about that mansion you live in? What about the clothes you wear? All the places you've traveled to?"

"I was an orphan," Lila started her story and even managed a tear in her left eye. "My parents worked as servants for the Fowler family and they both died in a car crash when I was one year old. The Fowlers kept me in their house

76

and as soon as I was eight years old, they put me to work."

"What do you mean, they put you to work?" Robby's eyes widened and his mouth dropped open.

"I cleaned for them and cooked for them. They had a little girl of their own named Venice who was a year younger than me so they used me as a playmate for her. Every time we'd play with her toys, I had to clean everything up. When the family would travel, Venice would go out with her parents to the fancy restaurants and museums and I would wait for them in the hotel room. I got Venice's old clothes although they were always too small for me. Still, I was grateful for what I got. I know I was lucky that they took care of me, but—" Lila broke off and made an expression as if what she was about to say was just too painful.

"But, what?" Robby asked, on the edge of his seat. "Please don't stop."

"To tell you the truth," Lila said, pausing and sighing for the maximum effect, "they weren't always very nice to me."

"What did they do to you?" Robby asked.

"They would send me to bed without any supper a lot," Lila said, wiping a tear away from her cheek. "Usually, Venice would do something wrong like break a vase or make a huge mess, and she would blame it on me. As we got older, she would smoke

77

cigarettes and hide the packages in my room even though I don't smoke. They always punished me for things that Venice did. After a while, I just gave up trying to convince them that it wasn't my fault."

Robby looked like he was going to cry. "Well, what's it like now? Are they still cruel to you like that?"

"It's better now that Venice is out of the house," Lila said. "She's at a boarding school in Switzerland. She didn't want to live with her parents anymore. She always complained about them. I don't think she ever realized how lucky she was to even have parents."

"Wow. I don't know what to say," Robby said. "It must have been terrible for you growing up in that atmosphere. There I was pretending to be a millionaire because I thought that's all you were interested in. I guess we have more in common than I thought. I feel terrible that you paid for that expensive dinner last night. How were you able to get the money for that?"

Good question, Lila thought. *Come on! Think of something quickly!* "Over the years, the Fowlers gave me a very small allowance. I never spent any of it, so I managed to save up a few hundred dollars in my piggy bank."

"So, you used part of your life savings to take me to dinner?" Robby asked incredulously. "I feel awful about that. That's just too amazing."

"Please don't feel bad," Lila said, smiling sweetly and pretending to be the most noble, self-sacrificing person in the world. "It makes me happy to give to other people. I decided a long time ago that if I was ever a millionaire, I would give all my money away to those who need it more."

"I had no idea," Robby said, drawing her closer to him. "I see you in a whole other light now. I have so much admiration and respect for you. You're truly a beautiful person." Robby kissed Lila passionately on the bench as the people walked by on the street.

Oh, no! Lila worried. *What if this plan backfires on me and he likes me even better poor?*

"Who wants ice cream?" Jessica asked at the Wakefields' dining-room table that Monday night. Sue and Jeremy were eating dinner with the Wakefields, and they'd been holding hands throughout the entire meal. Jessica thought she was going to scream if she had to sit there one more minute watching Jeremy look sadly and lovingly at the dying Sue. She had to get him alone so they could talk about what was going on.

"That's a great idea. There's some cookie-dough ice cream in the freezer," Mrs. Wakefield said. "And there's a delicious blueberry pie that Sue made. Jessica, honey, why don't you go get us some?"

"I'll help you," Jeremy said.

"So, did you tell Sue about us?" Jessica asked Jeremy in an urgent whisper once they were in the kitchen.

"Sue and I are going through with the wedding," Jeremy said slowly and gravely as he got the ice cream out of the freezer. He didn't even look at Jessica. "Because of Sue's illness—which I'm sure you probably know about, since Sue told me that she told your sister last night—I've decided that I can't leave her."

"But, what about us?" Jessica asked in desperation, fighting back the tears. "How can you just walk away from what we have together?"

"I know how you must feel," Jeremy said as he touched Jessica gently on her cheek. "I know you must be hurting right now but please understand my situation. Sue and I have a history together. How could I live with myself if I walked away from her at the worst time in her life?"

"Don't you think Sue would prefer you to be happy?" Jessica pleaded. "If she knew how you really felt, I'm sure she wouldn't want you to marry her."

"But she'll never know how I feel because I don't want her to," Jeremy said. "I want her last few years to be free of stress and pain."

"You and I love each other," Jessica cried. "We're supposed to be together. You have the right to be happy."

"Sometimes in life we can't only think of ourselves," Jeremy said. "What you and I have together is truly special and magical but we have to put that behind us. We have to do what's right, and putting our feelings for each other aside is the right thing to do. Also, Jessica, think about it. I'm twenty-three and you're sixteen. That's a really big age difference. It wouldn't be right for you to get serious at your age."

"But when I'm with you, I feel like we're the same age," Jessica pleaded. "Time and age have no meaning. I don't care how old you are, and I'm already serious about you. It's too late for me *not* to be serious about you."

"All of that's irrelevant now," Jeremy said sadly. "I'm going through with this wedding as we originally planned it."

"Won't the wedding be too much for her if she's so sick?" There must be something she could say to get Jeremy to change his mind. She had to make him see things her way. She couldn't let him get away.

"She wanted to call the wedding off but I wouldn't hear of it," Jeremy said. "I know she still wants to marry me, even if she only has a short time to live. I can't deprive her of her final wish. She wants the wedding to go on exactly as planned, and she said it's really important to her that your parents not know about her being sick.

81

She realizes how excited your mother is about the wedding and she doesn't want to take that away from her. Also, she wants the mood to be light and joyful. She's afraid people will treat her differently because she's sick. She's truly a strong and courageous woman."

Jessica looked at Jeremy, the most handsome man she'd ever seen in her life. She knew in her heart that they were soul mates and that they were meant to be together. She knew she would never, in her entire life, feel that way about anybody else. And that was why, at that moment, she felt a pain so severe that it cut through to the deepest core of her being.

Chapter 7

"I was thinking about making it a book shower," Elizabeth said. It was Tuesday afternoon and Elizabeth was at the Dairi Burger with Enid and Olivia Davidson. Elizabeth, trying her best to keep her mind off Todd, was planning a shower for Sue and she wanted her friends' input.

"What exactly is a book shower?" asked Enid, whose idea it had been to give Sue a shower in the first place.

"I read about it in one of the bride magazines Sue had lying around," Elizabeth said. "Instead of everyone bringing things the bride doesn't need, like egg slicers and lemon zesters, everyone brings a book. After all, you can never have too many books, I always say."

Enid rolled her eyes. "When you get married, I

83

will definitely throw you a book shower. In fact, for your next birthday, we'll tell everyone to only bring books. It's a great idea—for *you*. But, get real, Liz. I'm not sure books are what Sue has in mind. And speaking of books, I think maybe you should lay off them for a while."

"What do you mean by that?" Elizabeth asked.

"Well, it just seems like all you've been doing lately since you got back from London is read books," Enid said. "You need to lighten up. We're starting to worry about you."

"Enid's right," Olivia said. "This is summer vacation, after all. There's plenty of time to read when school starts up again in the fall."

"Just because it's the summer, I don't plan to let my brain turn to Jell-o," Elizabeth said. "And anyway, now that I've just stopped seeing Todd, I need my books to help me keep up my strength. In fact, today I just started one called, *Breaking Up Is Hard to Do: Ten Steps to Surviving Your Breakup*. It's been really useful."

"Well, getting back to the shower," Enid said, "I think most people prefer a more traditional kind of thing."

"Like what?" Elizabeth asked.

"Like kitchen supplies," Olivia suggested.

"Too boring," Elizabeth groaned.

"Too boring?" Enid repeated. "And this coming from the person who just suggested books."

"I went to a shower for my cousin recently and everyone brought her sexy lingerie," Olivia said, giggling. "Some of it was really nice and some of it was really suggestive."

"That does sound a little more appropriate," Enid said. "And it's a lot more fun to shop for than kitchen supplies and books."

"Do you really think that's a good idea?" Elizabeth asked, picturing the dying Sue in a red teddy.

"Of course it is," Enid insisted. "Don't be such a prude. It'll be fun."

"I just want Sue to be happy," Elizabeth said, looking down at her salad.

"Why wouldn't she be happy?" Olivia asked. "You're throwing her a shower and she's about to marry the stud of all studs."

Elizabeth couldn't tell them the real reason she was worried about Sue's happiness—that she was dying of an incurable disease and that her fiance was in love with Jessica. And she couldn't explain why she felt responsible for Sue's happiness. More than ever she just wanted to make the days leading up to the wedding the happiest of Sue's life.

The waiter brought over two enormous hot fudge sundaes, shaking Elizabeth out of her thoughts.

"Are you sure you don't want one of these?" Olivia asked Elizabeth as she plunged her spoon into the mound of whipped cream in front of her.

"The fudge is so hot, it's better than ever," Enid swooned.

"No, thanks," Elizabeth said, taking a bite of her salad. "I'm trying to stop eating chocolate or desserts of any kind."

"Why?" Olivia asked. "Don't tell me you're going to get all weight-obsessed and start dieting like Jessica and *her* friends."

"No, it's not really about weight," Elizabeth explained. "It's about control. The other night I ate almost half of a chocolate mousse cake by myself. I realized that I had no self-control."

"Who wants self-control?" Enid joked as she took a huge bite of sundae.

"In my love-addiction book, there's a whole chapter about food and how overeating is a sign of being too needy and dependent. It's like needing too much love. They say that everything you do in your life is a matter of making choices. Like being in control or out of control," Elizabeth explained.

"Well, I'd rather be *out* of control and eat this delicious sundae," Olivia said. Both girls laughed.

"It's not funny." Elizabeth's tone was serious. "If you can't control these impulses, then how will you control other impulses? Like if you're really mad at someone, what's to stop you from killing them?"

"I think you're taking this self-help thing too

far," Enid said. "This is exactly what I was talking about when I said you should stop reading so much. I'm sure there's a lot of good you can get out of these books, but keep it in perspective."

"Yeah, it's not as if we're going to all go out and kill people now that we've eaten hot fudge sundaes," Olivia joked.

"Well, when you've gained fifty pounds and your faces have all broken out with acne, don't come whining to me about it," Elizabeth said.

"I find your implication that Enid and I have weight and skin problems to be rather insulting," Olivia said.

"Really," Enid agreed. "You're taking all the fun out of eating this sundae," Enid said, pushing her half-eaten sundae away. "So, how 'bout it? Did we decide on the lingerie theme?"

"Yes, I guess so," Elizabeth said. *Maybe something frivolous and fun like a lingerie party is exactly what Sue needs to get her mind off of her problems.*

"Then let's go hit the stores," Enid said enthusiastically. "Our mission is to find the sexiest lingerie in Sweet Valley!"

"Hey guys! What are you doing here?" Jessica said to Sue and Jeremy in the sporting goods department of Lytton & Brown's store on Tuesday. She had overheard Sue on the phone that morning

87

making plans with Jeremy to meet there. Even though Jeremy had explained his determination the night before to go on with the wedding, Jesssica couldn't bear the idea of Jeremy and Sue spending time alone together, so she'd decided to make sure they didn't. Also, Jessica reasoned, if Jeremy spent more time with her, he'd realize how much he needed her in his life.

"We're looking for a tent to use on our honeymoon," Jeremy said awkwardly, looking down at the floor.

He can't even look at me because he knows that if he does, he'll get weak and have no choice but to call off the wedding, Jessica thought. *Well, I'll just have to make sure to spend as much time with him as possible.*

"This looks like a nice one," Jessica said, pointing to a tent on display.

"Jessie," Sue said, laughing, "that tent you're pointing to has two separate sleeping compartments."

"So it does!" Jessica exclaimed, trying to sound surprised. *Nice try*, she told herself.

"I don't think separate sleeping compartments are exactly what we had in mind. Right, sweetie?" Sue started to give Jeremy a big smooch when Jessica suddenly yelled out.

"Look at that one!" Jessica pointed to an enormous tent on the other side of the showroom just as their lips were about to touch.

"That could sleep an entire Boy Scout troop," Jeremy said, laughing.

His laugh and smile were the things Jessica loved best about Jeremy. She felt suddenly light-headed and weak, and she had an urgent need to be alone with him.

"We don't need anything too big," Sue said in that gushy, girly way that bugged Jessica. "In fact, the more intimate, the better."

Sue was working her way back to Jeremy when Jessica proposed an idea. "Sue," Jessica started sweetly, "I've been thinking about your kind offer to get something for my parents to thank them for the engagement party. And I think I know what they would like."

"Oh, Jessica, thank you! What is it?" Sue asked.

"It's on the fifth floor in the china department," Jessica said. "It's a big soup bowl with a ladle and it's in the shape of a big, red rose."

"That sounds perfect," Sue said. "Jeremy, honey, while I'm getting that bowl, why don't you go downstairs to the men's department and get yourself some new jeans?"

"Don't you think I should come with you?" Jeremy asked Sue. "After all, it's going to be from both of us."

"Don't be silly," Sue said. "You run along and get your jeans, and let me worry about the gift. It's a bride's responsibility."

Jessica wondered if Jeremy minded Sue's bossing him around like that. *Why does he let her tell him what to do?*

"Jessie, you'll come with me, won't you?" Sue asked. "That way, I'll find the exact bowl you're talking about."

"Actually, I need to do some shopping of my own," Jessica lied. "You won't have any trouble finding it. Believe me, it's an original."

"Then let's all meet in half an hour back at my car," Jeremy suggested.

Jessica walked with Sue and Jeremy to the bank of elevators and quickly jumped into the one with Jeremy. Luckily, there was no one else on it. When Jessica went to hit the button to go to the men's department, she pressed the emergency button instead, causing the elevator to stop between the floors. She did it so discreetly that Jeremy had no idea what she'd done.

"That's weird," Jeremy said. "We don't seem to be moving."

"Oh, no! Do you think we're stuck?" Jessica asked, trying to sound like she was panicking.

Jeremy pushed a couple of buttons, but the elevator still didn't move. Jessica noticed that Jeremy's brow was covered in sweat and he looked more nervous than she'd ever seen him. "I'm really sorry. I'm sure someone will be here soon. Are you OK?"

Jessica looked deeply into Jeremy's eyes. "I'm fine, although I *am* slightly claustrophobic," Jessica lied. "Would you mind holding my hand?"

Jeremy took Jessica's hand reluctantly; then, Jessica flung her arms around his neck. "Oh, Jeremy," Jessica said, unable to control herself, "I've been dying to be alone with you."

Jeremy pushed Jessica off of him, moved to the other side of the elevator and crossed his arms. "We can't do this, Jessica. I meant everything I said last night about going through with the wedding. I'm sure we'll be out of here soon, so let's just keep our distance and talk about something innocuous."

"I know you're still going through with the wedding and I respect that," Jessica said, moving toward him. "I just can't bear not being with you."

"This is the way it has to be," Jeremy said, moving away again. "We have to do the right thing."

"I don't want to do the right thing," Jessica said. "Sue will get to be with you every day. And if all I get is just a few stolen moments, then I'll take what I can get."

Jessica backed Jeremy into a corner of the elevator. They were standing right next to each other but they didn't touch. Jessica felt her whole body tingle with the excitement of being so close to him in this secret, stolen moment. And she thought it was thrilling that Sue was in the same department

91

store, totally unaware of what they were doing. Jessica knew she shouldn't be thinking things like that, especially since Sue was sick and everything, but she couldn't help it. *I don't care if we stay in here for hours or even days. I don't need food or anything else from the outside world as long as I'm with Jeremy.*

"Being together like this just makes it harder, and it's not fair to Sue," Jeremy said. "It only gives you hope for something that can't be. Not only do I feel guilty about what I'm doing to Sue, but I feel terrible about what I'm doing to you."

"But you're not doing anything to me," Jessica said. "You have nothing to feel guilty about as far as I'm concerned. It's not your fault that I feel this way about you, and you can't help the feelings you have for me. It just happened. It's nobody's fault."

"I feel like I'm leading you on, though," Jeremy said sadly. "I don't want you to end up hating me because of this."

"I could never hate you, but I *will* be mad at you if you don't do something," Jessica said coyly.

"What's that?" Jeremy asked.

"Kiss me," Jessica commanded, looking up at him seductively.

"Jessica, I really can't," Jeremy said weakly.

"Please," Jessica pleaded. "Nobody will ever know."

Jeremy hesitated for a moment, then pulled

Jessica toward him, kissing her with such passion that Jessica thought she might faint. Suddenly, the elevator bell sounded and the doors opened to an amused crowd of shoppers. Secretly, Jessica wished that Sue had been one of them.

"And here's your mother on the first day of school, freshman year," Mrs. Wakefield said, pointing to a picture in an old photo album. "From that very first day when your mother walked into our dorm room, I knew we'd be friends for life."

It was Tuesday evening before dinner, and Mrs. Wakefield was showing Sue pictures from her college days with Sue's mother. Mrs. Wakefield was sitting on the couch in the family room between Elizabeth and Sue, and Jessica was lounging on the floor, flipping through a fashion magazine.

"What a funny hairdo," Sue said, laughing. "I never saw my mom with hair like that."

"We all had funny-looking hair back then," Mrs. Wakefield said, turning to the next page in the album.

Jessica was pretending to read the articles so she wouldn't have to talk. All she wanted was to think about Jeremy and the last kiss they'd shared in the elevator earlier that day. Also, she couldn't help chuckling to herself when she recalled Sue's surprise and disappointment over not being able to find the bowl Jessica had described to her. Sue kept going on and on in the car ride home from the store about how if she'd only thought of it earlier, she would have bought the bowl before somebody else did. It took all of Jessica's self-control not to blurt out that there was never any bowl in the first place, just so she'd shut up about it. But Jessica didn't think Jeremy would be crazy about the fact that she'd lied to the poor, sick Sue in order to have a stolen moment with him.

"Who's that?" Elizabeth asked, pointing to a picture of her mother with her arm around a man she'd never seen before.

"That is Peter Mallard," Mrs. Wakefield said, touching the picture tenderly. "He was the reason your mother and I almost stopped being friends."

Jessica looked up from her magazine for the first time, curious about what her mother had just said.

"What do you mean, Mom? How did he almost ruin your friendship?" Jessica asked.

"Well, it's a long story, and anyway, our friendship turned out to be too strong to let some handsome young man come between us," Mrs. Wakefield said.

"Tell us about it," Sue urged. "I really love hearing about my mom when she was younger."

"Peter Mallard was a junior when Nancy and I were freshmen, and we thought he was the cutest thing we'd ever seen. He was on the football team and at the top of his class. We both met him at the same time." Mrs. Wakefield looked amused and wistful as she remembered her past.

"Where did you meet him?" Elizabeth asked.

"Nancy and I went to a fraternity party together and neither of us knew anyone else there. We were just standing together in a corner and Peter came up to us and started talking."

"And then what happened?" Jessica asked, sitting up on the floor. "Who did he like most?" Jessica, of course, was hoping he liked her mother best.

"Well, it was hard to know," Mrs. Wakefield said. "He was so friendly to both of us that I left the party thinking he liked me best, and Nancy left thinking the same thing."

"Go on," Elizabeth commanded impatiently.

"Neither of us wanted to tell the other one that we had a crush on Peter."

"Why not?" Sue asked.

"I knew your mother liked him and she knew that I liked him, so we both thought it best to keep quiet. Anyway, Peter asked me to go to the library to study with him the next week," Mrs. Wakefield said.

"That was your date?" Jessica asked making a face. "Talk about boring. That sounds like the kind of dates Elizabeth and Todd go on."

"Be quiet," Elizabeth snapped at Jessica. "So did you tell Sue's mother about your date?"

"No, I didn't tell her because I didn't want her

to be upset," Mrs. Wakefield explained as she looked lovingly at a picture of her friend. "I felt like she was a sister even after just knowing her for such a short time, and I didn't want to do anything to hurt our friendship."

"Did my mom ever find out?" Sue asked.

"Well, it turned out that Peter also asked your mother out that same week, and she didn't tell me about it," Mrs. Wakefield said, laughing.

"I never knew my mom was so sneaky," Sue said, obviously amused. "Was that it? Did you both just go out with him the one time?"

"No, we both kept going out with Peter for a while and we both kept it from the other one the whole time. Actually, I think this went on for almost two months."

"How did you keep it from each other?" Jessica asked. Jessica couldn't help seeing the similarities between her mother's story and what was happening to her right then.

"When I was going out with Peter, I would make up some story about having to go do a project for a class or something."

"So how did it all finally work out?" Elizabeth asked.

Just then, Mr. Wakefield walked in the room. "OK, my world-famous chili is served!" he announced. "I feel like I'm interrupting something. More wedding planning?"

Mrs. Wakefield smiled and winked at the girls. "Yes, just more wedding stuff. That's OK, though, we'll finish it another time."

As everyone left the room, Jessica walked over and looked at the album. People had always said that Elizabeth and Jessica looked just like their mother did when she was younger. As Jessica looked at the picture of her mother with Peter, she realized it was really true—Jessica felt like she could be looking at a picture of herself with a bad hairdo. When she flipped to the next page, she saw that Sue looked eerily like *her* mother, too. *Hmmm, I wonder which one got the guy? My look-alike or Sue's?*

Chapter 8

"Where did Sue go?" Jessica asked as everyone was sitting down to eat Mr. Wakefield's chili. "Isn't she eating with us?"

"No, she and Jeremy are going out for a pizza and then to a movie," Mr. Wakefield said as he scooped out big servings of chili into bowls. "I told her I'd save her some of my chili so that she could have it tomorrow. It is my secret recipe and it would be a shame for it to go to waste."

"I think it's nice for Jeremy and Sue to spend a little time alone together before the wedding," Elizabeth said, smiling at Jessica. Elizabeth couldn't resist the temptation to tease her sister about Sue and Jeremy. After all, it was time for her to start facing up to reality. "Don't you agree, sister dear?"

Jessica stuck her tongue out at Elizabeth.

"What's with you two?" Mrs. Wakefield asked. "You're acting like little girls."

"One of us is, anyway," Elizabeth said.

"Do you have any idea what movie they're seeing?" Jessica asked, ignoring Elizabeth's comment.

"Why do you want to know?" Elizabeth asked, although she knew exactly why her scheming sister was asking.

"I was thinking of going to a movie myself, if you must know," Jessica said snidely to her twin.

"I think they were seeing a documentary about rain forests," Mrs. Wakefield said. "Sue seemed really excited about it. Apparently, she and Jeremy had been hearing a lot about it, and they were pleased that it was playing at the Valley Cinema."

"I've really been dying to see that movie, too," Jessica said. "I love nature films."

"Since when?" Elizabeth asked.

"Just because we're twins doesn't mean you know everything about me," Jessica said, smiling at her parents. "I'm going to go see it after dinner."

"But don't you think Sue and Jeremy should be alone?" Elizabeth asked, looking sternly at her sister.

"I'll just sit in the back and they'll never know I'm there," Jessica said as she dipped a corn chip in her chili.

100

Then I'll be sitting right there with you, Elizabeth thought. At least if Elizabeth was there, the damage Jessica would wreak would be kept to a minimum.

"Shhhh," Elizabeth said to Jessica, who was coughing and rattling her popcorn loudly as they walked into the movie theater after the film had started. "Stop making so much noise."

"Stop telling me what to do," Jessica said. "It's bad enough that you followed me in the first place. Do you also have to monitor every little thing I do?"

"I *thought* you said you were going to stay in the back and keep a low profile," Elizabeth whispered tersely. "You're bothering everybody."

Jessica stood in the aisle and looked at the screen, which was showing a close-up shot of a black bug crawling on a tree. "I'm sure the audience needs a little livening up anyway if this is what they've been watching."

"Let's just sit here," Elizabeth whispered, pointing to two seats in the back row.

"No, I don't like to be so far back. I want to get a good look at that fascinating bug." Jessica walked farther down the aisle with Elizabeth sticking by her side like glue. Jessica stopped and scanned the rows in the darkened theater. Her eyes stopped moving when she found what she was looking for.

"Forget it," Elizabeth said when she saw that mischievous expression in her sister's eyes. Elizabeth grabbed Jessica's arm to keep her from walking toward Sue and Jeremy.

"Let go of me!" Jessica said, causing some nearby audience members to shush them. She jerked her arm away and started making her way down the row directly behind Jeremy and Sue's. Elizabeth, mortified, followed her evil twin.

Jessica sat in the seat right behind Jeremy, and Elizabeth had no choice but to sit behind Sue.

"I can't believe you're doing this," Elizabeth whispered in Jessica's ear. "Don't you have any self-respect? You're just embarrassing yourself."

"Quiet!" Jessica whispered back. "I'm trying to watch the movie. This is my favorite part." On the movie screen in front of them two monkeys were fighting over a banana.

Jessica was chomping loudly on her popcorn, and Elizabeth was hoping that Sue and Jeremy wouldn't turn around because of all the noise Jessica was making. Elizabeth didn't know what her sister was going to do, but she was anticipating the very worst. *Maybe she'll just leave them alone*, Elizabeth hoped, although she knew her twin better than that.

After about ten minutes had gone by, Sue lifted her arm and put it around the back of Jeremy's seat, resting her hand on his shoulder. Elizabeth looked over to see how her sister was reacting. *So far, so good*, she thought as she saw that Jessica was still just eating her popcorn and trying to pretend that she was interested in the movie.

A few more minutes went by and Sue leaned over to kiss Jeremy on the cheek. He turned and smiled at Sue, then they both went back to watching the movie, which even Elizabeth thought was incredibly dull. For the millionth time that day, she thought of Todd and how much she missed him and for the millionth time that day, she banished the thought from her mind. She looked over at Jessica again and was relieved to see Jessica was still happily munching her popcorn.

Just as Elizabeth was finally starting to relax, Sue turned toward Jeremy and pulled his face toward her own. She started kissing him on the mouth, and before Elizabeth realized what was happening, Jessica stood up, spilling popcorn all over Sue and Jeremy.

Elizabeth closed her eyes, wanting nothing more than to crawl down under her seat and run outside.

"I'm so sorry!" Jessica gushed loudly as Sue

and Jeremy turned around. "Jeremy! Sue! What on earth are you doing here?!"

"Jessica! Elizabeth!" Sue exclaimed amidst the shushing of the audience. "What a nice surprise. I didn't know you two were interested in rain forests." Sue and Jeremy were pulling popcorn out of their hair and brushing it off their clothes.

"We're not," Elizabeth said flatly.

"Liz isn't but I am," Jessica said. "Could we come sit with you guys?"

"Of course," Jeremy said, looking rather embarrassed.

"Actually, we're fine here," Elizabeth said as she kicked Jessica in the calf.

"You can stay where you are but I want to be closer to the screen." Jessica started to climb over the seats, forcing Sue to move over, and planted herself right smack dab in the middle of Sue and Jeremy.

"Well, I sure am glad I'm keeping Jessica out of trouble," Elizabeth said to herself.

"Who wants ice cream?" Jessica asked when the movie was over and everyone was standing in front of the theater.

"You really like ice cream," Sue said.

"What do you mean?" Jessica asked.

"It seems you're always going out for ice cream. How do you stay so slim?" Sue asked.

"Oh, you know. Exercise and all that . . ." Jessica said.

"Jessica, I think you and I should go home now," Elizabeth said. "I'm pretty tired and I'm sure Sue and Jeremy would like to be alone."

"Actually, we *were* thinking of taking a drive," Jeremy muttered nervously.

"That's OK," Jessica said, sighing heavily and pouting. "I'll just go to Casey's alone. Bruce is busy tonight, but maybe I'll run into somebody I know."

Sue looked at Jeremy and smiled. "We wouldn't hear of it. Let's all go have some ice cream. That sounds great," Sue said. "You don't mind, do you, honey bunch?"

"Well, I'm still pretty full from that pizza we ate before the movie," Jeremy said.

Jessica was trying desperately to get Jeremy to return her gaze but he refused. *I guess it's just too painful for him to look at me*, she thought.

"Come on, sweetie," Sue said, nuzzling up to Jeremy.

"OK," Jeremy said reluctantly. "But let's make it an early night."

"Oh, goody! Liz, you can take the Jeep, and I'll just ride with Jeremy and Sue."

"Why can't we just ride together in the Jeep?" Elizabeth asked.

"I thought you said you were too tired for ice cream," Jessica said.

"I suddenly feel wide awake and hungry," Elizabeth said, perking up.

Jessica knew that Elizabeth's sudden burst of energy was motivated by her desire to keep an eye on herself and Jeremy. Lately she was beginning to feel more like a Siamese twin than an identical twin.

Jeremy slid into a booth at Casey's, and Jessica immediately plopped down next to him, forcing Sue and Elizabeth to sit on the opposite side of the table. Everyone ordered a hot fudge sundae.

Elizabeth felt a little guilty after having lectured her friends about the evils of ice cream, but she felt like she didn't have a choice. After all, she needed some reason to be there. Besides, she was so anxious about what Jessica might do that she needed something sweet to help calm her nerves.

"Hi, Elizabeth." Elizabeth looked up to see Todd standing there, looking handsome and forlorn. Elizabeth couldn't bear to look at him.

"Hi," was all Elizabeth could say.

"I'm Todd Wilkins," he said as he offered his hand to Sue and Jeremy.

"Oh, it's so nice to meet you," Sue gushed. "I've heard so much about you. Why don't you join us?"

"I don't think that's a good idea," Elizabeth quickly said before Todd had a chance to sit down.

106

"Why not?" Sue asked. Elizabeth hadn't wanted to burden Sue with her trivial problems, so she hadn't told her that they'd broken up.

"Well, we're going to discuss the film and it wouldn't be fair to Todd since he hasn't seen it," Elizabeth said.

"That's OK," Todd said, looking into Elizabeth's eyes. "I need to get home anyway."

Elizabeth watched as Todd walked out the front door. She suppressed the urge to run after him and tell him she forgave him. *But he deceived me*, she reminded herself, pushing down the little voice inside her head saying she'd done the same thing to him.

"Great film," Jeremy said when all the sundaes were brought to the table. "Did you girls enjoy it?"

"I thought it was one of the best films I've seen all year," Jessica enthused as she smiled brightly at Jeremy.

"Oh, really?" Elizabeth asked. "What was your favorite part?" Elizabeth knew Jessica hated the movie, and she couldn't resist putting her on the spot.

"I liked the part about the butterflies," Jessica said as she dug her spoon into her sundae.

"I was really fascinated by the different medicinal herbs that were found in the rain forest," Sue said. "There are so many different cultures that use tropical remedies to cure all kinds of diseases."

Of course, that would be of particular interest to Sue, Elizabeth thought. *She's probably really interested in alternative medicine. Anything that could help keep her alive.* And once again Elizabeth thought how miniscule her problems with Todd seemed in comparison to what Sue was going through.

Chapter 9

"What are you giving Sue and Jeremy for a wedding present?" Robby asked Lila as they walked around the Sweet Valley Mall on Wednesday afternoon.

Lila made a dramatic face and sighed heavily. "I'm afraid I can't really afford to give them very much. I was thinking of just writing them a poem."

"I'm sure they'd love a poem," Robby said, putting his arm around Lila's waist as they walked. "I never knew you were a poet. I love poetry. Who's your favorite poet?"

"Who's my favorite poet?" She repeated the question. Lila was drawing a blank. Not only did she not *write* poetry, she didn't read much of it, either. She had read some poetry in school, but she couldn't come up with one single name.

"I think Robert Browning is my favorite," Robby said, saving Lila from an embarrassing moment. "He was such a romantic."

"He's one of my favorites, too," Lila lied. "William Wordsworth!" Lila shouted out excitedly, suddenly remembering the name of a poet. "William Wordsworth is my favorite!" She had studied him in her English class. Never before had she appreciated something she'd learned in school as much as she did right then.

"'I wandered lonely as a cloud—that floats on high o'er vales and hills,'" Robby started to recite a Wordsworth poem.

"'When all at once I saw a crowd—a host, of golden daffodils'!" Lila couldn't believe she was able to pull that line out of the recesses of her brain. *It's amazing what the human mind is capable of when faced with a gorgeous hunk*, she thought. Each student in her class had been required to memorize one poem and that was the one Lila had learned. Lila thought it was a miracle that that happened to be the poem that Robby started to recite.

"I like Wordsworth, too," Robby said. "And I think it's really sweet that you want to write a poem for Sue and Jeremy."

"I feel terrible about not being able to give them a proper gift," Lila said, returning to her poor orphan demeanor. "It's really embarrassing."

"How about if we buy something together that could be from both of us?" Robby offered.

"That's really nice of you, but I'm afraid I wouldn't even be able to pay for half of anything that would be acceptable." Lila stared off in the distance, looking wistful, and for a minute she almost convinced herself of her impoverished state.

"Look, why don't I pay for a gift and we'll just say it's from both of us?" Robby said. "I'd really like to do that for you."

"You're too kind," Lila said like a noble heroine. "But I would never be able to repay you and I'd just feel too guilty being in debt to you like that."

Robby stopped walking and turned to face Lila. He pulled her toward him and gave her a big hug. "Lila, I can't tell you how close I feel to you. You're so unselfish and generous. And even though your childhood was about a million times harder than mine was, our backgrounds are much more similar than I'd ever imagined."

"I feel really close to you too, Robby," Lila said, overwhelmed by guilt. He was so moved by thinking that she had suffered as a child when really she was the wealthiest girl in Sweet Valley who had everything she'd ever wanted.

"I have to confess something," Robby said, pulling away and looking incredibly serious. "When I first met you I was intimidated because I thought

111

you were so wealthy and from such a different world than me. I thought it would be impossible for us to ever really connect. Maybe I've become a reverse snob over the years, but I don't have a high opinion of people who have had life handed to them on a silver platter. I believe in hard work and paying dues. And you've certainly paid yours."

Lila was mortified. Her plan to get back at Robby had gone way too far. Now it would be impossible to let him find out the truth about her. He would never want to talk to her again. *Why did I ever start this ridiculous thing? I've worked myself into a corner that I'll never be able to get out of!*

"These look perfect," Mrs. Wakefield said to Sue and Elizabeth. She was pointing to bouquets of peach and white sweetheart roses at the florist. The three of them were choosing bouquets for the bridesmaids and the bride. "I think they would look great with Jessica and Elizabeth's dresses."

"Those *are* lovely," Sue agreed. "I'm going to see what's in the cooler there."

"Don't you think you should let Sue decide about the bouquets herself?" Elizabeth whispered to her mother once Sue was out of earshot. "After all, it *is* her wedding. If you're so adamant about a certain flower, she'll think that's what she'll have to choose even if she doesn't like it."

Mrs. Wakefield looked at her daughter with a

puzzled expression. "I'm just making a suggestion. She doesn't have to do what I say. I'm just being helpful."

"Well, I think we should let her find what she likes, and then you can give your opinion if she asks for it," Elizabeth said. Elizabeth wasn't in the habit of telling her mother what to do, but at that moment she was more concerned about Sue's happiness than anything. She knew Sue wanted to please her mother—that was just Sue's sweet way—and she didn't want her mother to have undue influence on Sue's choices.

"Here's a beautiful bridal bouquet," Sue called across the shop.

"Now, even if you don't like it," Elizabeth whispered to her mother as they walked toward Sue, "act really enthusiastic about it."

Mrs. Wakefield turned and looked at Elizabeth. "Aye, aye, sir," she said, laughing.

"I'm serious," Elizabeth said.

"I can see that," Mrs. Wakefield said.

Elizabeth, Mrs. Wakefield, and Sue stood in the cooler, looking at the roses. Sue had found a bouquet that had big lavender and pink roses in it, mixed in with baby's breath.

"I think this is just so beautiful," Sue said. "The roses look so healthy and hopeful."

Elizabeth thought she was going to cry right there in the cooler. She was so moved by Sue's comment about the roses. Sue wasn't healthy, but she was drawn to the roses because they were. She *was* hopeful, though. How she managed to keep up her optimistic, cheerful spirit was a mystery to Elizabeth. Elizabeth knew she would never be able to stay so pleasant about everything if she were in Sue's shoes. "That certainly is a gorgeous bouquet," Mrs. Wakefield enthused. She looked over at Elizabeth as if to ask whether or not she'd given the appropriate response.

As they continued to walk around the shop, they passed by the big funeral wreath displays. *I should have directed us in a different direction*, Elizabeth scolded herself. She didn't want anything to make Sue think about death. Elizabeth looked at Sue to see if she noticed them. If she did, she didn't show it. *I wonder if she thinks about death all the time. It's just all so tragic. I wish I could do something to keep her from being sick. I'm trying to control everything else, but that's the one thing I can't do anything about.*

Chapter 10

Thursday morning Sue and the Wakefields were eating breakfast in the Wakefields' kitchen. Sue had made her special French toast for everyone, and Jessica was purposely not eating any. She couldn't get the idea out of her head that Sue would be waking up every morning, making breakfast for Jeremy. She looked at Sue as she walked around the kitchen, so perky and happy, and Jessica had an overwhelming desire to tell her the truth about Jeremy just so she could wipe that cheerful expression off her face.

"Doesn't the French toast taste right to you?" Sue asked Jessica. "You've barely touched it. This was my mother's recipe. She made it every Saturday morning when I was little."

"I think I'm just going to have an English muffin," Jessica said. "I'm not really crazy about French toast."

"Jessica, you *love* French toast. What are you talking about?" Mrs. Wakefield asked with surprise.

"I used to like it, but I guess my tastes have changed as I've gotten older," Jessica said dramatically. Jessica just felt like being difficult. She knew Elizabeth was giving her one of her disapproving looks, but she refused to acknowledge it.

"I'm sorry," Sue said. "I didn't know you didn't like French toast. I thought everyone liked it."

"Don't worry about it," Jessica said, trying to use a tone that would make Sue feel guilty.

"Well, I think this is the best French toast I've ever had," Elizabeth gushed. "French toast is definitely one of my favorite foods. Isn't it great, Mom?"

"Yes, it is," Mrs. Wakefield agreed. "Delicious."

"So, what's everyone doing today?" Mr. Wakefield asked as he put down the newspaper he'd been reading. "It looks like a beautiful day out there."

"Jeremy and I are going to Project Nature up the coast to take a hike and do a little volunteer clean up," Sue said as she helped herself to another big piece of French toast. *She certainly has a healthy appetite for a dying woman*, Jessica thought to herself. "I'd love to help," Jessica said enthusiastically. "I'm in the mood for a hike today."

"Did I hear you correctly?" Elizabeth said, pretending to get something out of her ear. "Did you just say you're in the mood for a hike today and you'd love to help clean up?"

"Yes, you heard me correctly," Jessica snapped at her sister.

"I don't think Sue meant that they were taking a hike around the mall," Elizabeth teased. "And I don't think she meant they'd be cleaning out the clothing stores by buying everything in sight."

"Very funny," Jessica said sarcastically.

"I think that's terrific that you want to help us," Sue said brightly. "We need all the help we can get. You'd be surprised at all the garbage that's left behind by the campers that go there."

Jessica was imagining sneaking off to a little glade in the forest with Jeremy. She'd leave the garbage pick up to Sue. Also, she wanted Jeremy to think that she was interested in the same things he was. It still bothered her that he and Sue had common interests. She'd show him that she was just as interested in the environment as Sue was. Most importantly, Jessica wanted to spend as much time with Jeremy as possible before the wedding. There were only two days left, but she still hadn't given up hope that things could turn around in her favor.

"It is such a gorgeous day," Elizabeth said, looking out the kitchen window, "that I think I'll come along for a hike as well."

Jessica was fuming. She'd had enough of her sister following her around like a shadow. She wished Elizabeth would just let her live her own life. "I thought you were going to spend the day getting ready for Sue's shower," Jessica grumbled. "And didn't you want to help Mom with the wedding preparations?"

"I don't have much to do for the shower," Elizabeth said.

"And I think we're actually in pretty good shape for the wedding," Mrs. Wakefield said. "I'm going to be at the office all day today anyway, so there wouldn't be anything for you to do. But now, Sue, are you sure you and Jeremy don't mind Jessica and Elizabeth tagging around with you today? Don't you two lovebirds want to be alone?"

Jessica cringed in her seat. Her mother had just made her feel like an eight-year-old kid. *It's really Sue and Elizabeth who will be tagging around me and Jeremy*, she thought. *We're the real lovebirds.*

"It's wonderful that Jessica and Elizabeth want to join us. The more the merrier!" Sue enthused. "And besides, we'll have plenty of time to be alone together on our honeymoon."

Jessica was in her bedroom, searching frantically for the perfect hiking outfit with which to dazzle Jeremy. Luckily, she had some tight-fitting khaki shorts that showed off her figure. She

118

put on her white silk blouse that she always felt great in, and a pair of tan sandals that made her feet look sleek and sexy. She was brushing her hair when Elizabeth flung open the door to her room.

"Hurry up! Sue and Jeremy are waiting in the car!" Elizabeth announced. "This isn't a ball we're going to by the way. You're going to be picking up trash and walking in the mud, so it doesn't matter what you look like. Those sandals are totally impractical. And don't you think you should really be wearing a T-shirt instead of a silk blouse?"

"For the one thousandth time—stop telling me what to do and what not to do!" Jessica said. "I'm really getting sick of it. Now, I know why you're going on this hike today, and I'm not happy about it. But since you insist on going, I want you to mind your own business and let me do as I please."

"Jessica, I'm only looking out for you," Elizabeth said. "I just know that the more you entertain this crazy idea about you and Jeremy being together, the more difficult it's going to be when he's married. You have to wake up and smell the espresso!"

"No, *you* have to wake up and smell the espresso," Jessica quipped back. "My life is my life—and your life, as boring as it might be, is your life. You can't control what I do. And you don't have to keep rubbing in the fact that he's getting married. I'm not

119

an idiot. I'm very aware that he's getting married."

"Look." Elizabeth drew in a deep breath. "All I'm saying is just leave Jeremy and Sue alone. Today, for instance, don't try anything like you did at the movie the other night."

"What are you talking about?" Jessica said as she sprayed herself with perfume.

"I'm talking about the little accident with your popcorn," Elizabeth said. "Now, let's go. You look fine. I'm sure the bugs in the forest will be very impressed."

"OK, here's the plan," Jeremy said as he knelt down on a dirt path, spreading out a map. "Sue and I will head out in that direction." Jeremy pointed to a path on the left.

"Won't I be going on the same path with you guys?" Jessica asked as she slapped a mosquito off her arm, then leaned down to scratch her leg.

"No, you and Elizabeth will go down that path," Jeremy said, pointing to a path on the right.

"But why aren't we all going on the same path?" Jessica asked.

"Because we'll get more accomplished if we split up. We'll end up at the same place and we'll have a picnic," Jeremy said, smiling nervously at Jessica. "Here are your bags." Jeremy handed them enormous green plastic garbage bags.

"What are these for?" Jessica asked.

"They're for picking up the trash, of course,"

Sue said, putting her arm around Jeremy. "Oh, and they're recycled."

"Oh, I'm so relieved," Jessica said. "I was just going to ask that."

Elizabeth found it somewhat amusing that Jessica was not only going to be picking up garbage but that she was going to be separated from Jeremy. At the same time, though, she couldn't help feeling a little sorry for her sister, who looked hot and uncomfortable standing in the woods with her silk blouse on.

Jessica smacked another mosquito off her face. "Isn't anyone else getting bothered by the bugs?"

"I bet it's all that perfume you're wearing," Sue said. "I should have told you not to wear any today."

Jessica and Elizabeth headed down their path with their garbage bags. Elizabeth was actually happy to be walking in the woods. She loved nature walks and was happy to have any excuse not to think about Todd.

"You just passed by a soda can," Elizabeth said to Jessica.

"You pick it up," Jessica hissed. "I'm not touching that disgusting trash and getting germs all over me."

"But I thought that was the point of this trip," Elizabeth said. "You might as well get into the spirit of it. It will help pass the time while you walk."

"Forget it," Jessica said. "Trash collecting is not

my thing. Besides, I doubt we'll be walking for too long anyway."

"Jessica," Elizabeth started, "I'm afraid you're in for a surprise."

"What are you talking about?" Jessica asked, moving her hair out of her face.

"I heard Sue and Jeremy say something about this being a six-mile hike," Elizabeth said.

Jessica stopped in her tracks. "You're kidding, right?"

"No, I'm not kidding," Elizabeth said as she bent down to pick up a hamburger wrapper.

"Well, I'm going back to wait in the car," Jessica stated. "You can clean up the garbage by yourself."

"Don't you think Jeremy and Sue will think it's a little strange that you're just giving up on the hike so soon? After all, Sue did tell us that we'd be hiking and picking up trash. I'm sure you wouldn't want Jeremy to think you just came along to be with him."

Jessica didn't say anything but just continued walking down the path, angrily slapping at mosquitoes and refusing to pick up any garbage.

"This is absolutely horrible," Jessica said after twenty minutes had gone by with neither sister saying anything to each other. "I've never been more miserable in my life. I'm itching everywhere, there are bugs flying in my mouth and ears, and I'm so hot and thirsty I think I'm going to faint."

"Why don't you put all that out of your mind

and look around you. Just try putting mind over matter," Elizabeth said, stopping to smell a wild flower. "It *is* beautiful here, after all. Just listen to the quiet of the woods and the birds singing."

Elizabeth looked at her sister. Jessica's face was bright red, her legs were covered with scratches, and her white silk blouse was splattered with mud. She did look miserable. "Would it help if we sing as we walk?" Elizabeth asked.

"Thanks for the suggestion, Mary Poppins, but I think if you start singing right now I will have to kill you," Jessica said. Elizabeth shrugged her shoulders and they continued walking in silence.

After what seemed like hours, Jessica decided that there was no possible way she could walk another step. And she was dying to see Jeremy, alone. *That was the whole reason I went on this stupid hike*, she thought to herself. Suddenly, she had an idea.

"Ouch!" Jessica cried. "Liz! Wait up! My foot!" Jessica was sitting on the ground, holding her foot and making a pained expression.

Elizabeth walked back to her sister and knelt down. "What happened?"

"I was walking along and I guess I tripped on something. I'm in terrible pain. I can't walk anymore," Jessica said.

"We're almost there," Elizabeth said. "I think we only have about five more minutes until we get to

123

the picnic place. I've been following the markers as we've been going along. What if I just help you the rest of the way. You can lean on me for support."

Jessica forced a tear from her eye. She'd perfected the art of crying on demand over the years. It was a skill that often came in handy. "I just can't do it, Liz," she said in a little voice. "I think you should go get Jeremy and have him come back and carry me to the top."

Elizabeth started to hold Jessica's ankle for closer inspection when Jessica let out a loud "OUCH!"

"Please," Jessica said, putting on the water works and rocking back and forth. "I'm not kidding. I really think I broke something."

"OK, OK," Elizabeth said, obviously concerned. "I'll be right back. Maybe they brought a first-aid kit or something."

"I really think you should just send Jeremy back. I'm going to need to be carried and you're not strong enough."

"Maybe you're right," Elizabeth conceded. "Don't try to move and don't be scared."

It worked! Jessica thought happily. Jessica knew that no matter how suspicious Elizabeth might be of her, she hated for Jessica to be upset or hurt. She was lucky Elizabeth loved her so much, especially in times like these.

Once Elizabeth was out of sight, Jessica stood up

and flipped her hair over, letting it fall back on her shoulders. Whenever Jessica didn't have a brush handy, she used the flip-over method to puff her hair up a bit. *Just like a good Girl Scout!* she thought. She pulled her lip gloss out of her shorts' pocket and put some on her lips. She tried to wipe the mud off her shirt, but she decided it was a lost cause.

She heard footsteps on the path, and she quickly sat back down on the ground. She grabbed her foot with both hands and summoned up another tear. She rubbed just a little bit of dirt on her face, thinking that would make her situation seem just a bit more dramatic.

"Jessica! Are you OK?"

There he was. His bright blond hair was shining in the sunlight that fell on the path through the trees. He was out of breath and looked so rugged and handsome that Jessica thought she might faint right there from sheer attraction.

"I'm so sorry," Jessica said as Jeremy sat down next to her.

"Why are you sorry?" Jeremy asked, brushing her hair out of her face. "I'm the one that's sorry for bringing you here in the first place."

"I'm sorry to have ruined your hike," Jessica said, looking into his eyes that were darker than ever. "I think I might have broken my foot."

Jeremy took Jessica's sandal off, ever so gently, and held her foot in his hands. "Does that hurt?" Jeremy asked as he touched her foot in different places.

Jessica winced. "Yeah, it does, a little bit."

"Luckily, Sue packed some ice for our picnic," he said as he put an ice-filled bandana on her ankle. "You probably just twisted your ankle. You're lucky. It doesn't seem to be swelling up. We'll keep it on your ankle for a little bit, then I'll help you get up to the top. We're not far at all."

"Thank you, Jeremy," Jessica said, kissing him on the cheek. Jeremy jerked his face away from Jessica.

Their eyes locked and for the first time Jessica became aware of the sounds of the birds singing. She heard the rippling of a brook nearby, and she was overcome by her love for Jeremy.

Neither of them had to say anything. They both knew what the other was feeling and thinking. Jessica put her arms around Jeremy and put her head against his chest.

"We can't do this," Jeremy said, starting to move back but unable to pull himself away.

"Shhh," Jessica said, putting her hand on his mouth. "Don't say anything." *Just let yourself feel how much you need me. You'll see that we're meant to be together like this forever!*

Chapter 11

"Who brought the patties?" Robby asked as he stirred around the charcoals. "We're ready to throw on the meat."

Sue and Jeremy had organized a barbecue on the beach Thursday night. They invited their friends who had come in from out of town, and they told Jessica and Elizabeth to invite their friends as well.

Jessica was so exhausted after her hike in the woods that day that all she wanted to do was collapse into a hot tub and stay there for the rest of her life. As tired as she was, though, she wasn't about to miss an opportunity to be with Jeremy. She didn't even care that there would be other people there. At least she could see him and he could see her.

Jessica was wearing her favorite new, silk mini-dress with spaghetti straps. It was white and had little lavender and yellow roses on it. It showed off the perfectly bronzed tan she'd finally given in to. When she'd first gotten back from London earlier that summer, she'd wanted to cultivate a sophisticated European pallor, the way the English did. But after just a few days in Sweet Valley, she'd given that up and quickly regained the summer tan look that she thought looked best on her.

When she got ready for the party that night, she was feeling more beautiful than ever. Her face looked red and rosy from hiking in the sun, and the good feelings she'd gotten from spending those precious moments with Jeremy were radiating from her whole being.

"Are you going somewhere after the cookout?" Lila asked Jessica. Jessica was sitting with Lila and Amy Sutton on a blanket on the sand. The sun was going down, and one of Jeremy's friends was playing a guitar nearby.

"No, I'm not doing anything afterward. Why do you ask?"

"It's just that you look so fancy," Lila said. She flipped her hair to the other side then smiled at Robby who was throwing burgers on the grill. "What's the special occasion?"

"Earth to Jessica," Amy teased. "You look like

you're back in London—definitely not in the same country with the rest of us."

"What are you talking about?" Jessica asked, throwing off her sandals.

"Lila just asked you what the special occasion was," Amy said as she stuck her hand in a bag of pretzels.

"Do I have to have a special occasion to look nice?" Jessica barked. "I never knew it was a federal offense to wear a dress. I'll be sure and call the fashion patrol the next time I get dressed."

"Hey, take a chill pill," Lila said.

"I'm going to grab a burger before they're all gone," Amy said. "And Jessica, you look really pretty tonight, by the way."

"Thanks," Jessica muttered.

"What's with you?" Lila asked once Amy was gone. "Jeremy?"

"Yeah, I guess I still can't get used to the idea that he's marrying Sue," Jessica said, looking over at Jeremy, who was telling some story to his friends, making everyone laugh. In the past, Jessica had told Lila every last detail about every single date. But with Jeremy it was different. She wanted to savor what happened between her and Jeremy, keeping it all to herself.

"What's going on with you and Robby?" Jessica asked, trying to change the subject. "You guys were looking pretty cozy walking down the beach just now."

129

"Well, things look great and he thinks everything's great but—"

"But what?" Jessica said. "What happened to your plan to get back at him?"

"That's the problem," Lila said, sighing. "He likes me even more now that he thinks I'm poor."

"Are you sure he's not just pretending to like you more? Do you really think he believes your story about being a poor orphan?"

"He definitely believes it and I'm so convincing that sometimes even I believe it," Lila said.

"Well, just go home tonight and look inside your closet, and then you'll remember that you're not exactly a poor orphan," Jessica teased.

"I feel so guilty about lying to him like that," Lila said. "And I really don't think he's going to want to see me anymore if he finds out the truth."

"Am I hearing what I think I'm hearing?" Jessica asked. "Correct me if I'm wrong, but I seem to remember that he pretended to be something he wasn't and you forgave him. I think you've forgotten what the whole point of your plan was in the first place."

"I feel like I *have* forgotten the point," Lila said. "I meant for it to just be a game, but I think it's gone too far now."

"If I were you, I wouldn't give up yet," Jessica

said. "You're just doing the same thing to him that he did to you."

"I guess you're right," Lila said, a doubtful expression on her face.

When Jessica got up to get a hamburger, Sue called her over to sit on a blanket with Jeremy and their friends.

"Jessica, that's such a cute little dress you're wearing," Sue said. "Are you going on a date with Bruce later?"

Jessica felt her face turning crimson. She looked at Jeremy who caught her gaze. "No," Jessica said, "I just felt like sprucing up a bit after that hike."

"Your ankle must be better," Sue said. "You don't seem to be having much trouble walking around on it."

"Yeah," Jessica said uncomfortably. "It must have just been a temporary muscle thing."

"What do you do, Jessica?" their friend, Sally Haskins asked. Sally worked with Sue and Jeremy at the Project. She had long, curly brown hair and was wearing big beaded earrings and lots of bracelets. She looked like she would work at the nature conservancy, Jessica thought—more so than Sue did with her nice designer clothes and neat haircut. Jessica had noticed Jeremy talking to Sally for a long time earlier in the evening. She looked really cool and sophisticated, and Jessica couldn't help wondering if Jeremy was attracted to her.

What is wrong with me? Jessica thought. *I'm never jealous like this.*

"Jessica's still in high school," Sue said. "Isn't that adorable?"

There's that horrible word again! Just don't let her get to you, Jessica told herself.

"I wish I were still in high school sometimes," Sally said. "There's no rent or phone bills to worry about. All you have to think about is where the party is on Friday night."

"That feels like a lifetime ago," Sue said. "Jessie, you should really appreciate this carefree time in your life."

Carefree? Yeah, right, she thought. *The only way I'll be carefree is when I get Jeremy all to myself.*

"So what do you all think of the new parks commissioner in California?" Andy Green asked. Andy was one of their friends from the East Coast. Jessica thought he was sort of cute with his long, curly hair. But he was dressed like he was stuck in the 1970s with a tie-dyed shirt and leather choker.

"I don't feel like I've been here long enough to have a really informed opinion," Jeremy said. "He seems to be on the right track, though, especially with his opposition to offshore drilling. He put up a really big fight against the oil companies."

"Well, Jessica's the only real Californian sitting here," Sue said. "What do you think about him?"

Jessica didn't even know the name of the commissioner let alone any of his policies. "I think his policy of putting coke machines and video screens in every park is pretty great," Jessica joked. *When in doubt, make a joke!* Jessica was pleased to see that everyone, including Jeremy, was laughing at her joke.

As the conversation about California politics and environmental policy continued, Jessica felt as if she had nothing to add besides the occasional joke. Jessica always had something to say no matter what the conversation was, but now she felt as though she didn't belong. For the first time since she'd known him, she felt younger than Jeremy. She felt like Jeremy and Sue shared a whole world that she knew nothing about. She remembered seeing the article the two of them had written together for a nature magazine and how envious she'd been at the time.

Bruce and Pam Robertson, Bruce's real girlfriend, arrived at the barbecue together, and Sue gave Jessica a sympathetic smile. Sue leaned toward Jessica and whispered, "I'm so sorry. I guess it didn't work out with you and Bruce."

"Yeah, I guess it just wasn't meant to be," Jessica said. She got up and walked down the beach by herself. *Sue probably thinks I'm walking off because of Bruce. Fine, let her think what she wants*, Jessica thought. She had to get away from Sue and their friends. The closer she was to Jeremy, the harder it was not to want to throw her arms around him.

"You look great tonight," Todd said to Elizabeth as he tentatively sat down next to her in the circle around the fire. Andy and Bruce were playing their guitars and everyone was singing along.

Elizabeth was wearing her new jeans and a sleeveless blue denim shirt. Her hair was hanging down freely around her shoulders. Usually, she pulled it back in a ponytail or a barrette, but tonight she'd decided not to bother. She knew she looked beautiful but she didn't care. All she cared about was trying to ignore the feelings that were rising up in her from Todd's nearness. She was determined not to be drawn in by his presence. *Stay in control*, she repeated to herself.

Elizabeth stood up to move away from Todd, ignoring the beseeching look he gave her as she left. *If I keep a physical distance from him, then I won't risk weakening my resolve not to get back together*, Elizabeth decided. She walked to the other side of the circle and sat down with Sue and Jeremy. "Hey, Sue, have you seen Jessica?"

"I was just worrying about her," Sue said. "She headed off down the beach. And I'm afraid she left because of Bruce and Pam."

"Bruce and Pam? Why would she— Oh. Right. Bruce and Pam."

"She looked pretty upset," Sue said. "Jeremy, honey, be a love and go bring her back."

"It's really not necessary," Elizabeth protested loudly. "She probably really just wants to be alone."

"Well, it would make me happy if she were here with all of us," Sue said. "Will you just go bring her back, Jeremy?"

Elizabeth watched as Jeremy stood up. "I'll go get her. We'll be back in a flash," Jeremy said.

Well, you better be or I'll just have to come and bring you both back! Elizabeth thought.

Jessica was walking down the beach, listening to the roar of the waves and imagining she heard them calling her name. She continued walking, but when she heard her name again she turned around and saw Jeremy running toward her in the moonlight. Her heart stopped. He'd followed her. He was feeling the same desperation

135

to be with her as she was to be with him.

"Hey, are you OK? You looked pretty upset back there," Jeremy said.

"I'm fine," Jessica said softly, turning her back to him so he couldn't see her face.

"I know how difficult this must be for you, seeing me with Sue," Jeremy said, coming up behind her and putting his hands on her shoulders. "But this is the reality now, and the sooner you start accepting it, the easier it's going to be for you."

"But I refuse to accept it," Jessica cried, turning around, seeing his strong face reflecting the moonlight. She felt the waves circle around her feet in the sand. "You know you're supposed to be with me."

Jeremy started to put his arms around her but she pushed him away. "Don't," she said. "You can't have it both ways!"

He looked at her with a hungry intensity and she knew he was dying to kiss her. This was exactly what she wanted—to make him want her, to have him realize that no matter how hard he tried, he couldn't resist her.

Jeremy leaned in toward Jessica, and just as she was deciding whether or not she would let him kiss her, Elizabeth made the decision for her.

"Yoo-hoo! Hey, guys!" Elizabeth yelled to Jessica and Jeremy and waved. She couldn't tell from where she was standing, but it looked like they were just about to kiss. *Phew! I got here just in time*, Elizabeth thought.

"I really feel silly coming after them like this," Enid said. "I hate getting involved in these things. It's really none of our business what they do."

"It is too our business," Elizabeth said as she pulled Enid by her sweatshirt toward the two figures in the distance. *Jessica*. Elizabeth was still irritated at Jessica for the stunt she'd pulled earlier in the day when they were hiking. She couldn't believe she'd been gullible enough to believe that Jessica had really hurt herself. She should have known that Jessica was just trying to maneuver a moment alone with Jeremy. After they'd eaten their picnic, Jessica's foot was miraculously better, and she'd had no problem walking back down the mountain.

"Hey, you guys," Elizabeth said when she and Enid had reached them. "You're missing a great party."

"Yeah," said Enid, obviously uncomfortable, "your friend Andy is a really good singer, Jeremy."

"Yeah, come on," urged Elizabeth. "Sue's waiting," she said pointedly.

"You guys go," Jessica said, sending darts with her eyes at her sister. "We'll join you in a little while."

137

"Maybe we should go back," Jeremy said, obviously embarrassed about being caught by Elizabeth and Enid. "I want you to hear Andy play."

"You and Enid go back," Jessica said. "I need to talk to my sister."

Once Enid and Jeremy were gone, Jessica turned to Elizabeth and crossed her arms in front of her. "I hope you're satisfied. You're keeping me from being happy. Is that what you want? Are you getting pleasure out of making my life miserable?"

"Jess, I'm just trying to protect you," Elizabeth said.

"Protect me from what? A werewolf? It seems to me that you're the one who needs protection. If you'll remember London, you're the one who goes out with dangerous guys. Not me."

"That's not fair," Elizabeth said, amazed that Jessica could be so insensitive.

"Well, it's not fair to keep me and Jeremy apart," Jessica said. "You're not my mother and you're not my guardian and you're not my bodyguard. You're certainly not acting like my friend or my sister."

That hurt. It was because she *was* trying to be her friend and sister that she wanted to protect Jessica. Why couldn't Jessica understand that she was just as worried about Jessica getting hurt as she was about Sue having her heart broken? *Why does she have to twist everything around and see my motives in the worst way?* Elizabeth thought as they walked back to the barbecue in silence.

Chapter 12

"Jessica, you really should put on some sunblock," Elizabeth said. "You know all that sun isn't good for you."

"I always tan," Jessica said, lifting up her head. "I never burn. And my policy has always been that if you build up a tan gradually, then you don't peel or blister." Jessica was lying on her stomach on a lounge chair by the Wakefields' pool, playing the memory of the night before over and over again like a movie. Except in her movie, Jeremy kissed her, and Elizabeth and Enid didn't show up and ruin the moment.

When Elizabeth, Sue, and Mrs. Wakefield came out to have some iced tea by the pool, Jessica was less than thrilled. She felt as if her special thoughts were being invaded by their presence.

"It doesn't matter if you tan or burn," Elizabeth said, sitting down at a table next to Jessica's lounge chair. "You can still get skin cancer and wrinkles."

Jessica looked up at her sister. "Who are you? The surgeon general? You're the one who's going to end up with premature wrinkles from scrunching up your face and worrying about everybody else all the time." Jessica burrowed her head in her crossed arms that served as a pillow and covered her face with her hair.

"We just worked out the seating arrangement for the dinner reception," Mrs. Wakefield said, ignoring the girls' bickering. "We could use your help writing out the place cards, Jessica."

Jessica looked up again and saw that they were all three sitting at a table, writing busily on little cards. "Maybe in a while," Jessica said. "My hand's kind of sore today."

"What's wrong with it?" Sue asked.

"I don't know. Maybe I hurt it when I fell down yesterday on the hike," Jessica lied.

"Jessica, I seated you next to our friend Andy," Sue said giddily. "I think he had a little crush on you last night. He *is* a little old for you, but still, he's awfully cute and I think you might really like him."

"Great," Jessica groaned. *This is what my life is destined to be like from now on*, she thought. *People are going to set me up with their friends or*

142

brothers, hoping I'll like them when really there's only one guy on the planet for me. The thought sent her into a deeper depression. But then something occurred to her that hadn't before. *If Sue is telling the truth, and she really does have this rare blood disease, then she'll be out of the picture in a couple of years and Jeremy and I can be together then.* She shook her head as if to banish the evil thought from her head. *Besides,* she thought, *I don't want Jeremy by default. I want him the first time around!*

The possibility of that happening, though, was getting more and more slim. Jessica looked around at the Wakefield yard, which was already set up with tables and chairs for the wedding reception. When Jessica first saw the set up, the reality of the wedding hit her like a ton of bricks. The moments in the moonlight with Jeremy the night before seemed more like a dream. That's why she had to keep remembering all their moments together— she had to remind herself that they hadn't been a dream. *These memories are going to have to last me a lifetime if I can't be with him.*

"Hey, Mom," Elizabeth said as she neatly wrote out names on place cards, stirring Jessica out of her thoughts. "You never finished telling us what happened with you and Sue's mom and that guy."

"That's right!" Sue enthused. "Who ended up with Peter?"

Jessica turned over and propped up her lounge chair to a sitting position. This was a story she didn't want to miss.

"Well, where did I leave off?" Mrs. Wakefield asked as she refilled the glasses with iced tea from a big glass pitcher.

"You were telling us that you and Sue's mom were both dating Peter for a couple of months without the other one knowing," Jessica piped in, eager to hear how the story turned out.

"That's right," Mrs. Wakefield said as her face lit up. "And since we were always wearing each other's clothes, we found out later that we'd even worn the exact same outfits on our dates with him."

"So how did you finally find out that you were both seeing him?" Elizabeth asked.

"One night Nancy and I had gone out together to get a pizza at a restaurant in town. We sat down at a booth in the back and after a little while, Peter walked into the restaurant, hand in hand with a girl neither of us had seen before. They sat down at another booth and Peter didn't see us. We were both upset about it but neither of us let on. Finally, after we each got more and more agitated watching Peter and his date giving each other goo-goo eyes—"

"Goo-goo eyes?" Jessica teased. "Is that what you all said back then?

"Yes, that's what we said back in the dark ages."

Mrs. Wakefield laughed. "Anyway, neither of us was eating our pizza. We just kept staring at Peter and his date. Then, at the same time, we both let down and confessed that we'd each been dating him."

"Did you all have a fight?" Jessica asked.

"That was just it. Instead of fighting, we both started laughing and we got even closer because of it. We decided that the only thing to do was to get even," Mrs. Wakefield said.

"And how did you do that?" Sue asked.

"First we put on lots of red lipstick, then we walked over to his booth and fawned all over him in front of his date. We both planted big kisses on his cheeks, then we sat down at the booth with them. His face was covered with red lip marks. We went on and on about what fun we'd both had on our dates with him. I'd never seen anyone more embarrassed in my life." By this time, everyone was laughing.

"And what about his date? What did she do?" Elizabeth asked.

"She was so mad at him that she walked out of the restaurant with us. We left that three-timing cad alone with his pizza. And his date, Melody, became one of our best friends."

"So neither one of you ended up with Peter?" Jessica asked. She was disappointed by the story. She wanted her mother to have ended up with him.

"Nope. And neither of us wanted to after we

145

found out what he was really like," Mrs. Wakefield said.

Well, Jeremy isn't like that cad, Jessica reassured herself. *He's just the victim of a terrible situation.*

"I think you could get arrested for wearing that," Enid said as Sue held up a very revealing red satin negligee. It was Friday night, the night before the wedding and Elizabeth had organized a shower for Sue. The girls were sitting in the Wakefields' living room, and everyone was laughing about the lingerie. Everyone except Jessica.

"I'm sure Jeremy will like that one," Amy Sutton said. "It's such a pretty color and all," she said jokingly.

Sue pulled out a black lace teddy and held it up to her. "What do you think?"

"It's definitely you," Lila said. "I figured black goes with everything. Although, I guess you won't exactly be wearing it with anything else." All the girls giggled as they passed it around and took turns holding it up.

Jessica was sick to her stomach. The image of Sue wearing that teddy with Jeremy was unbearable. It didn't even help knowing that Jeremy really loved *her*. The fact was that he was marrying Sue and there would be no escaping a wedding night with Sue. The jealousy Jessica felt was overwhelming. It was all she could do to keep herself from grabbing the teddy and ripping it to shreds.

"How will I ever decide which one to wear on my wedding night?" Sue asked excitedly.

Jessica couldn't help noticing how happy and perky Sue seemed during the party. Her cheeks looked rosy and she didn't seem to be the least bit tired. Jessica thought she was acting pretty lively for a dying woman. *What am I thinking?* Jessica caught herself in mid-thought. *What if she really is dying?*

"Here's another present you didn't open yet," Elizabeth said, pulling a box out from under the table. "After tonight, you'll have to start a lingerie boutique."

Sue opened up the box and pulled out three pairs of oversized, white cotton underpants. She held them up and had a confused expression on her face. She opened the card to see who they were from.

"Jessica," Sue said, obviously surprised but forcing a smile. "Thanks a lot. They're really nice."

Jessica felt Elizabeth's angry eyes peering at her, but she refused to acknowledge them. "I thought you might want something practical," Jessica said. "You can never have too many pairs of cotton underwear, I always say."

"I guess you can wear those on the nights that you and Jeremy are having a fight," Sally said.

147

"Or you could use them as place mats," Enid joked. "Maybe even as a tablecloth. They're certainly big enough." Everyone, except for Jessica and Elizabeth, laughed.

"Well, they will be good for the cold nights when Jeremy and I are up in the mountains," Sue said, trying to make Jessica feel better. Little did she know that she was only making her feel worse and eradicating any feelings of pity Jessica might have briefly been feeling toward her.

I guess they will travel together, Jessica thought sadly. *They'll do all kinds of fun things together. Things that he and I will never do.*

Toward the end of the evening, the girls had moved out to sit by the pool. "Robby's throwing a bachelor party for Jeremy tonight," Lila said. "I don't know what they're going to do, but I'm sure it will be something pretty wild."

"Gross," Elizabeth said, making a face like she'd eaten something sour. "They'll probably have a woman pop out of a cake or show disgusting movies. It's so barbaric. In one of my new books, *Women as Seen Through the Eyes of Male Society,* the writer talks about the objectification of women over the years and about age-old sexist rituals like bachelor parties. Also, come to think of it, it's pretty sexist that the father of the bride gives the daughter away to the groom. It's like giving one man's property over to another."

"I'm actually glad to have my stepfather give me away," Sue said. "At first I didn't think he'd be able to get away from his business trip, but he just called last night and said he'd be here tomorrow."

"Oh, I'm so glad he can make it," Enid said. "That would have been a shame if he wouldn't be able to come after paying for the whole wedding and everything."

"He's not paying for it," Sue said quickly. "Jeremy is."

"Well, anyway, I still think bachelor parties are prehistoric," Elizabeth stated.

"Lighten up, Liz," Jessica said. "It's just a bachelor party."

"That's so typical for a woman to defend the behavior of a man," Elizabeth said. "I've been reading about how women always make excuses for the men in their lives rather than speaking up for their own needs. Like battered women who think everything is their fault, or women married to alcoholics who say their husbands need to drink to ease their stress."

"We're not talking about alcoholics or wife beaters," Jessica said. "We're talking about a few guys getting together—just like we are—to celebrate the last days of somebody's bachelorhood. I think we're all a little tired of your self-help books now."

149

"Well, I for one wouldn't mind knowing what the guys are up to," Lila said. "I don't exactly feel comfortable with the idea of Robby looking at a bunch of women running around in bikinis."

"I have an idea," Elizabeth said. "Let's raid the party."

"Are you serious?" Olivia asked. "You don't think they'd be furious if a bunch of girls appeared at their stag party?"

"Let them be furious," Elizabeth said excitedly. "I think it's a great idea." Even though Elizabeth knew that Todd would be at the party, she still wanted to go. Also, she had to admit that she couldn't stand the idea of Todd seeing a bunch of women in bikinis.

"So do I," Jessica chimed in.

Elizabeth looked at her twin, who was suddenly more animated than she'd been all night. *The only reason Jessica wants to raid the party is so she'll have one last chance to be with Jeremy before he's married. She better not pull anything at the party. If she tries—I'm going to stop her.*

"All in favor of raiding the party raise their right hands," Elizabeth said.

Everyone raised their hand except Sue and Sally.

"Count me out," Sally said. "That doesn't really sound like my speed."

"What about you, Sue? Aren't you curious to

see how Jeremy's going to spend his last night before the wedding?" Lila asked.

"I trust Jeremy completely," Sue said. "Besides, I think I'm going to want to get a good night's sleep before the big day tomorrow."

Of course, Elizabeth thought to herself. Elizabeth remembered that she was sick and weak and that probably even being up late at the shower was tiring her out. Sue had been such a good sport about getting into the sprit of opening all her presents. Elizabeth was pleased that the shower seemed to put the rosiness back in Sue's cheek. She had tried to do something to raise Sue's spirits and it had worked. *This lingerie shower turned out to be a good idea after all*, Elizabeth thought triumphantly.

"Hey, I have a great idea!" Jessica enthused. "Let's dress up!"

"Dress up like what? The bachelor party police?"

"Better than that! Like bachelor party bobbies!"

Chapter 13

"So, where are the girls?" Bruce asked as he looked under the table, expecting to find bikini-clad women. "Are you saving up the fun for when we cut open the cake and find a gorgeous girl inside?"

Robby had invited a group of guys over on Saturday night for a dinner party to celebrate Jeremy's last night of bachelorhood. He'd cooked since the crack of dawn, preparing an elaborate gourmet meal, which they were just sitting down to. He thought a quiet dinner party would be more appropriate than a rowdy blow-out considering what Jeremy had confided to him about Sue's illness. Robby had just taken a cooking course, and he thought that a sophisticated dinner party would be a nice alternative to the traditional bachelor party. But now he was starting to think it wasn't such a good idea. Most of the guys seemed pretty disappointed. They'd been expecting a wild night—not a quiet dinner by candlelight.

"Did you rent a nature documentary about rain forests to really top off this wild evening?" Steven asked, joking.

"We could go out dancing later," Bruce said as he shoved a huge piece of quiche in his mouth. "I know a pretty cool place where a lot of babes go."

"We could always go bowling," Todd suggested. "That might liven things up a bit. What do you think, Jeremy? It's your party, after all."

"What? Oh, yeah, anything sounds fine," Jeremy said. He had been playing with the food on his plate, not really listening to anything the guys were saying.

"Hey, Mr. Bridegroom," Robby said, noticing his friend's despondent behavior. "How 'bout you give me a hand with these dishes." *Poor guy*, Robby said. *He's probably just feeling sad about Sue.*

Jeremy got up and followed Robby with plates in hand.

"Hey, man, you look like your dog just got hit by a bus," Steven said quietly to Todd at the table. "We *are* at a bachelor party. You're supposed to be having fun. You've been moping around all night."

"To tell you the truth," Todd started, "it's about your sister."

"I know. I'm so sorry. I couldn't believe it when she told me you guys had split up."

"You're telling me," said Todd, eager to confide in Elizabeth's brother. Steven had been in a serious relationship with his girlfriend, Billie, for a long time now, and might be able to offer some advice. "I'm just so messed up about it. I know she loves me and I'm crazy about her. I did something really stupid, though, and I wish I could take it all back."

"What did you do?" Steven asked. "Elizabeth wouldn't talk about it."

"I had a little fling with some girl this summer, and I told Elizabeth about it," Todd said. "The dumb thing is that I really didn't like the girl that much—nowhere near as much as I like Elizabeth. It was a big mistake."

"Look, I've known Elizabeth for sixteen years, and she is the most stubborn person I've ever met," Steven said. "When she makes up her mind about something, she sticks to it. Lately, though, she's been really weird. She's so bent on controlling everyone and everything that she's not acting on her feelings. If I were you, I would remind her how she feels."

"But she doesn't want to have anything to do with me."

"That's just a front, believe me. Talk to her. You owe it to her to help her through this."

"I'm really sorry about the way this party turned out," Robby said to Jeremy in the kitchen as they scooped the second course, salmon mousse, onto the plates.

"Believe me, if I were at one of our old frat parties right now, I'm afraid I'd be in the same mood," Jeremy admitted.

"Is it just a case of cold feet?" Robby asked. "Or is it that Sue's so sick?"

"No . . ." Jeremy paused then continued. "I might as well tell you what's going on. I feel so guilty and confused—"

"You better tell me what it is," Robby said. "That's what best friends are for, you know."

"I'm not in love with Sue," Jeremy confessed. "I tried to be, but I'm not. I'm in love with somebody else."

Robby dropped the serving spoon onto the floor. "Who is it?"

"Jessica Wakefield," Jeremy said, letting out a big breath of air. "Ever since I met her on the beach that day, I can't think of anything else. And the worst part is, she feels the same way about me."

"And you have to go through with the wedding because of Sue's illness," Robby said sadly.

"Right. I have to marry her. How could I possibly abandon her now?" Jeremy asked.

"Whoa, I see what you mean. That's pretty heavy stuff," Robby said. "I'm sorry for Sue, of course, but this must be ripping you apart. Does Sue have any idea?"

"She doesn't know anything and I want it to stay that way," Jeremy said. "She's in enough pain as it is. I feel guilty about Jessica too, though. I led her to believe that I was going to call off the wedding and that we would be together. That was before I found out about Sue being sick."

"Well, I won't say anything to anyone about it," Robby said. "You can count on me. Now, we better get this next course out there before the guys fall asleep." On his way out of the kitchen Robby added, "And, Jeremy—"

"Yeah?"

"I'm here for you, man," Robby said.

"I know that," Jeremy said, smiling sadly. "That means a lot to me. And it means a lot to me that you'll be standing up there with me as my best man."

Robby and Jeremy carried the trays of salmon mousse back to the table and passed the plates around. Steven's eyes were closed, Todd was reading a book, and Bruce was playing tic-tac-toe with Andy.

"It's a joke, right?" Andy said. "Tell us what you

have planned. You were putting some knock-out in the cake just now, weren't you?"

This is the last time I'll ever throw a bachelor party, Robby thought to himself. *The guests are asleep, the bride is dying, and the groom is in love with another woman. Some party! Now, all we need is an earthquake to really finish off the night!*

"Police! Police! Freeze! This is a raid! You're all under arrest!" Jessica, Elizabeth, Lila, Olivia, Amy, and Enid burst into Robby's house dressed up like English bobbies, carrying billy clubs, and wearing moustaches and little blue hats, replicas of the real things that Elizabeth and Jessica had picked up at Heathrow on their way back from London.

"So, where are they?" Elizabeth asked, twirling her billy club around in the air.

"Where are who?" Todd asked, with a bewildered expression on his face.

"The girls!" Lila shouted.

"What girls?" Robby asked. "We're just a bunch of lonely guys sitting around eating mousse. We were just about to call it a night."

"Oh, right, you expect us to believe that?" Elizabeth walked toward the kitchen and raised her voice. "The party's over in there," she shouted at the kitchen door. "You can all come out now!" She swung open the door and stood

158

there with her mouth agape. "I bet they ran out the back door."

"Unfortunately, there really weren't any girls here," Bruce complained. "The food was great and everything, but I had more fun at my last dentist appointment."

"Is that really true?" Lila asked Robby. "There really weren't any girls here?"

"Cross my heart and hope to die," Robby said.

"Then I guess we seem pretty silly busting in here like this," Lila said.

"Actually, I'm thrilled," Robby said. "This is just what this party needed. Let's dance!" Robby turned on his stereo and everyone started to dance in the living room.

"I'm really glad you're here," Robby said to Lila as they danced close together to a slow song. "You look pretty cute in a moustache."

Lila tore off her moustache and gave Robby a kiss. "So, you cooked for all these guys? Do you cook a lot?"

"I love cooking. I just took a course in French cuisine. I'm pretty good, if I may say so myself," Robby boasted. "What about you? Do you cook?"

Lila almost burst out laughing from the absurdity of the question. She had never cooked anything in her life—she didn't have to, as the Fowlers had a full-time cook. Also, she and her parents

159

went out to fancy restaurants a couple of times a week.

"I love to cook," Lila lied. "I've been cooking for the Fowlers a lot over the years. Their daughter, Venice, had very specific eating habits, so I got pretty good at making unusual things."

"Really?" Robby asked excitedly. "We really do have a lot in common. I'd love for you to cook for me some time."

"You would?" Lila muttered quietly.

"You bet! How 'bout tomorrow?" Robby asked.

"But the wedding's tomorrow," Lila said. *Thank goodness!* she thought.

"The wedding's not until early evening," Robby said. "You could make brunch for me tomorrow morning."

"That sounds great," Lila said hesitantly. *What have I gotten myself into? I don't even know how to scramble an egg!*

"What are you looking at?" Steven asked Elizabeth, who was barely paying attention to her dancing. Everyone at the party was dancing except Jeremy and Jessica. They were both standing at opposite sides of the room by themselves. Elizabeth kept looking at Jessica, trying to send her a telepathic order to stay away from Jeremy.

"Our sister," she answered, sighing deeply. "I feel like I'm watching a bomb about to go off."

"What's she up to now?" Steven asked.

"She still hasn't given up on the idea of being with Jeremy, I'm afraid," Elizabeth said. "Not even the fact that he's getting married tomorrow is deterring her."

"Does Sue know?" Steven asked.

"No, she doesn't, thank goodness," Elizabeth said. She was on the verge of telling Steven about Sue's illness so he'd understand how truly terrible the situation was, but she knew she should respect Sue's wish for privacy.

"Well, as of tomorrow, he'll be a married man and there won't be anything Jessica will be able to do to come between Jeremy and Sue," Steven said.

"I just hope she won't pull anything between now and then," Elizabeth said. "When that ceremony is over and Father Bishop says, 'I now pronounce you husband and wife,' I'll finally be able to get a good night's sleep."

"Maybe instead of worrying about Jessica's love life, you should be worrying about your own," Steven said as he stopped dancing.

"What's that supposed to mean?" Elizabeth asked.

"I just had a little talk with Todd and he's a hurting pup," Steven said. "I think you should give the guy a break."

"And why should I give him a break?" Elizabeth asked. She looked over at Todd, who was

161

dancing awkwardly with Enid while looking at Elizabeth the whole time.

"Because he's nuts about you and he doesn't give a hoot about that girl this summer," Steven said.

"He told you about her?"

"Yes, and he told me it was a big mistake," Steven said.

"Well, I don't care what he says," Elizabeth said. "I'm happier not being in a relationship anyway. I feel more in control now than I ever have. Relationships just make you forget yourself and do stupid things."

Steven took Elizabeth by the shoulders and looked right into her eyes. "Listen, little sis, Todd's a great guy and sometimes even great guys make mistakes. I think you owe it to him to give him another chance. You only live once, and if you go through life always making rules and trying to be in control, you might miss all the good stuff that makes life worth living. Sometimes it's scary to go with your feelings but you can't be afraid to love."

"Gee, I never knew you were so deep," Elizabeth teased.

"Stick around your big brother and you'll learn all kinds of deep stuff," Steven said as he walked away from Elizabeth.

Elizabeth stood on the dance floor thinking about what Steven had just said. Even though she'd made fun of him, his words struck a chord with her. *We do only live once*, she thought, thinking about poor Sue and how she was going to spend her last years with the man she loved. *I guess I have been afraid to let myself feel anything. I could be hit by a bus tomorrow, and I wouldn't have let Todd know how I really feel about him.*

"Mind if I cut in?" Elizabeth said to Enid, tapping her on the shoulder.

Todd turned to Elizabeth, looking completely bewildered. Elizabeth and Todd started dancing to a slow song, holding each other close.

"Elizabeth, you have no idea how happy I am to be dancing with you right now," Todd said, pressing his cheek against her hair. "I wish I could take away all the bad feelings I caused you. If I had it to do all over again, I would never have had that silly thing over the summer."

Elizabeth laughed and felt suddenly lighter and happier than she'd felt in a long time. "I've decided to let you go free for good behavior." Elizabeth pulled off her moustache and kissed Todd on the lips.

"I should have more affairs from now on," Todd said when he came up for air.

Elizabeth gave him a gentle punch on the arm. "No, you shouldn't. No more flings. For you *or* for me. Todd, I'm a total hypocrite. I had a thing with a guy in London."

Todd stopped dancing and looked at Elizabeth in disbelief. "Are you joking?"

"Unfortunately, I'm serious," Elizabeth admitted. "It turned out to be a total nightmare. His name was Luke and he *really* turned out to be something different than he appeared. In fact, he turned out to be a total nutcase. He thought he was a werewolf, and he went around killing people. But that's a long story I'll tell you some other time."

"Did he hurt you? Where is he now? Did you really like this guy?" Todd asked all at once, his voice full of fear and concern.

"I liked him a lot at first because he was really into poetry and literature and stuff. He never hurt me and he never will because he's dead," Elizabeth said sadly.

"What a terrible thing for you to have to have gone through," Todd said, holding Elizabeth close to him.

"Let's just put it all in the past and think about right now," Elizabeth said.

"I guess it's normal for us to have little flings like that when we're apart," Todd said, pulling Elizabeth closer to him. "It's not like we're married or anything. And besides, maybe we're both more sure of our feelings for each other now."

"I realize now that I was just using your little

daliance as an excuse not to be with you," Elizabeth said. "I guess I was just afraid of getting hurt again."

"Enough about Luke and what's-her-name. Let's get back to Elizabeth and Todd," Todd said.

Elizabeth and Todd kissed on the dance floor until the past was far from their thoughts.

When Elizabeth came up for air, she looked at Jessica and then at Jeremy. They were both looking at each other with such longing that Elizabeth felt a moment of pity for her sister. *They really do look like two people who are truly in love.*

Elizabeth wasn't the only one who noticed the way Jeremy and Jessica were gazing at each other. Robby walked over to Jeremy and put his hand on Jeremy's shoulder. "Hey, man, it's torture just watching you watching her," Robby said. "Why don't you two get out of here for a while. I'll cover for you."

"But you went to all this trouble to throw this party for me," Jeremy said. "I'd feel bad just leaving like that."

"I'd rather you leave with Jessica and be happy, than stay here and look miserable. You two only have this one night to talk about stuff and be alone. Go for it," Robby urged.

Elizabeth watched as Jeremy walked across the room and led Jessica out the front door. She looked around the party and saw that nobody other than she and Todd saw them leave together.

"Well, aren't you going to go after them?" Todd asked.

Elizabeth stopped dancing and stared off into the direction of the front door.

"I'm tired of being a policewoman," she declared, throwing off her hat and billy club. "I'm just going to worry about myself from here on out."

"What are you talking about?" Todd asked, obviously confused. "I thought you were going to keep Jessica away from Jeremy. I thought you were really upset about the two of them being together."

"Steven just made me realize that I'm not responsible for what Jessica does." Elizabeth pulled Todd close to her to dance to a slow song. "I can't control anybody except for myself. The more I was trying to control Jessica, the more frustrated I got. Jessica and Jeremy are going to do whatever they want to do. I can't physically stop them. From now on, I give up controlling other people."

"Does this mean I'm no longer under arrest?" Todd asked, playfully.

"You're no longer under arrest, but you are under strict orders to kiss me," Elizabeth said, happier than she'd been in ages.

❖   ❖   ❖

Elizabeth floated up the stairs on the way to her room. She felt such a sense of relief after telling Todd about Luke, and she was thrilled that she and Todd were back together.

"Hey, Elizabeth, come on in for a minute." Sue was sitting on her bed, and her door was open when Elizabeth passed by.

The sound of Sue's voice immediately deflated Elizabeth's triumphant mood. *Just because I've given up trying to control everything, there are still things that are absolutely horrible, like Sue being sick and Jeremy being out with Jessica.* Elizabeth was hoping Sue would be asleep and she'd be able to avoid a discussion about the evening. *Just act normal,* she told herself. *Just act like everything's fine.*

"How was the party? Was it as wild as you thought it was going to be?" Sue asked.

"No, apparently it was a pretty boring evening until we showed up," Elizabeth said. "The guys were just sitting around the table, eating a quiet meal. There weren't any women running around in bikinis or jumping out of cakes. It was the exact opposite of what I'd imagined."

"Well, I hope Jeremy still enjoyed himself," Sue said. "It is his last night as a single man, after all."

You can bet he's enjoying himself right now, Elizabeth thought. *Enjoying himself in the arms of my sister.* She was trying as hard as she could not to let herself get all worked up about Jessica's deceitful behavior again. It was harder though, now that she was face to face with Sue. *Let go, let go, let go*, she kept telling herself. *Jessica and Jeremy are together right now, but there's nothing I can do about it. Just take care of yourself.*

"Where's Jessica?" Sue asked innocently. "Didn't she come home with you?"

Thanks, Jessica. Once again I have to lie for you to keep you out of trouble, Elizabeth thought. She looked at Sue, who seemed even paler and weaker than ever. She hated lying more than almost anything and especially lying to a dying person. "She and Bruce went out to the Dairi Burger for a late-night snack," she said, trying to sound convincing.

"That's nice that she and Bruce patched things up," Sue said.

"Uh-huh," Elizabeth uttered awkwardly.

"I'm actually glad the party didn't last that long," Sue said. "I don't want Jeremy falling asleep at the altar tomorrow." Sue laughed and Elizabeth forced a chuckle.

"How are you feeling?" Elizabeth asked.

"I'm OK," Sue said, looking down and sighing heavily. "I'm just a little tired."

"Are you nervous about tomorrow?" Elizabeth asked. *I certainly am, and you should be, too*, she thought.

"I thought I'd be really nervous like all the brides you see in movies and TV," Sue said. "But to tell you the truth, I'm surprisingly calm. I guess it's because I'm so sure about what I'm doing tomorrow. I'm marrying the most wonderful man in the world with whom I'm madly in love. And the best part is that I know he's madly in love with me. It's truly remarkable that he still wants to go through with the wedding even though he knows about my illness. He's the most unselfish man in the world."

Elizabeth was biting the inside of her mouth, trying to keep herself from yelling out, *He's not that wonderful and he happens to be incredibly selfish! In fact, he's spending the night before your wedding with another woman named Jessica Wakefield! But he's a grown man and I can't stop him. Whatever happens tomorrow is out of my hands!*

"I promised you a sunrise and here it is," Jeremy said to Jessica as they sat on the banks of Secca Lake. The sky was different shades of pink and orange, and the colors were reflected in the water. "I will remember you and this moment for the rest of my life."

Jessica was wishing with all her might that something could happen to change destiny. *How can he marry Sue? It's not fair. We were made for each other. Jeremy is the person who was created for the sole purpose of marrying me.* She was trying to be strong, but she couldn't hold back the tears.

"I'm sorry," she apologized as Jeremy wiped away her tears. "I just feel so sad. I've never felt so sad in all my life."

Jeremy pulled Jessica's face toward his own with his two hands and kissed each tear away tenderly. "I do love you, Jessica. I've loved you since the first time I saw you at the beach. Your golden hair was shining in the sun, and you radiated hope and optimism about life—things I hadn't felt since I was much younger. You're so young and beautiful, and you have your whole life in front of you. You'll fall in love a dozen times, and you'll find the man who will love and appreciate you for all your beauty. I just can't be that man."

"I won't fall in love again. I know that. And stop saying that I'm young. I don't feel young. I don't want to be with any other man," Jessica said, burrowing her face into Jeremy's chest.

"You feel that way now, but believe me, that will change. You'll go off to college and you'll be beating the men away with billy clubs," he said, lifting up Jessica's club and smiling.

"I don't care about college or other guys or anything else in the world besides you," Jessica said as new tears started to fall.

"Don't say that," Jeremy insisted. "I'm sorry. I'm so terribly sorry for all the pain I've caused you. Maybe in another lifetime, we'll be together."

"But I want to be together in *this* lifetime," Jessica cried. "If two people are meant to be together, then they should be together no matter what." This was Jessica's last chance to change Jeremy's mind, and she would do anything to keep him from walking down that aisle.

"Sometimes there are circumstances in life that are bigger than us—that we have no control over," Jeremy said, stroking Jessica's hair. "I honestly believe that even though we won't be together physically, we'll always be together in our hearts. I believe that true soul mates can wander around different parts of the world but they're always together. You'll always be with me, and I know I'll always be with you."

They kissed as the sun came up and Jessica trembled in his arms.

Chapter 14

"Jessica! Wake up!" Elizabeth was bouncing on Jessica's bed. "Today's the big day. We have a lot to do."

Jessica opened one eye and looked at the clock. "Go away," Jessica said as she hid her head under her pillow.

Elizabeth grabbed the pillow and pulled the covers off of Jessica.

Don't say anything about Jessica staying out all night with Jeremy, Elizabeth said to herself. *Just bite your tongue and keep your thoughts to yourself. You can't control other people. It will all be over by the end of the day. Just think about Todd and the first dance you promised him.*

"Come on, Jess," Elizabeth insisted gently. "Sue is expecting us to spend the day helping her get ready for the wedding."

173

"This is going to be the worst day of my life," Jessica groaned as she lay motionless on the bed. "I'm spending it in bed. Just tell everyone I'm sick. Tell them I have an incurable, rare blood disease."

"That's not even funny. That's totally sick-o," Elizabeth said.

"The last thing I need right now is a lecture," Jessica said.

"I'm not going to give you a lecture," Elizabeth said. "And I'm sorry I've been so bossy lately. I realize that what you do is your own business. But I do want to remind you that it's too late for you to try to change anything today."

"There are still a few hours left until they're actually married," Jessica said, suddenly sitting up straight in her bed.

Elizabeth hoped that Jessica was just trying to scare her with that comment. Unfortunately, Jessica had that look in her eye that Elizabeth knew too well. It was the look that signaled when Jessica was up to some new scheme.

Part of Elizabeth wished Jessica *would* just spend the day in bed. She felt in her bones that Jessica was still plotting some horrible thing to ruin the wedding. *Maybe she'll kidnap Jeremy, or tie Sue up and disguise herself as the bride and marry Jeremy!* She was fighting the overwhelming urge to lock Jessica in the closet. *Stay calm. Don't panic,*

174

she told herself. She felt like this would be the longest day of her life.

"What happened in here?" Robby asked Lila when he came into his kitchen from watching a baseball game on TV. "It looks like a disaster area."

Lila, trying to make waffles for brunch, was covered with flour and so were the floors and counters. Pots and bowls were turned upside down and there were eggshells all over the place. Lila looked completely worn out.

"Nothing happened," Lila said, wiping flour off her face. "Everything's fine. You just go back to the living room and leave the cooking to me. I always make a mess like this when I cook. It's just part of my creative process."

"Are you sure you don't want a hand?" Robby offered. "I hate for you to have to go to so much trouble."

"No, really, I'm very happy in here," Lila lied. "You just run along and I'll let you know when it's ready."

"OK, but just yell if you need me," Robby said as he left the room.

How do people do this? Lila thought as she looked at the mess around the room. *This is the hardest thing I've ever done. It's so much easier just to run out to a restaurant and buy this stuff.*

What's the point in going to so much trouble for something that's gone as soon as you eat it?

Lila was trying to smooth the lumps of flour in the bowl with the milk, but she couldn't get rid of the chunks. She figured it was just supposed to be like that, and that they would disappear once the waffles cooked a while. She tried to pick out the pieces of eggshell that had fallen into the batter but she lost her patience. *They'll probably go away, too*, she reasoned.

When she finally poured the mixture into Robby's waffle maker, she felt an enormous sense of accomplishment. She stacked all the pots and bowls in the sink and used almost an entire roll of paper towels to clean up the flour. She thought she smelled smoke, so she went over to the waffle cooker. Smoke was coming out of the machine, and batter was oozing down the sides. She opened it up and pulled something that resembled waffles out with a fork. She put the waffles on two plates and threw a handful of strawberries on top of each plate. *There, now they'll look pretty and I'm sure they'll taste just fine*.

"Brunch is served," she announced proudly as she carried the plates into the dining room. She was beaming with pride as Robby sat down at the table.

"This is really great," Robby said before he took

his first bite. "You're really terrific for cooking for me like this." He leaned over and gave Lila a little kiss on the cheek. "I hope it wasn't too much trouble. I was starting to feel a little guilty for asking you to cook for me."

"It was no trouble at all," Lila said, pushing the hair out of her face. "I love cooking."

Robby lifted his fork and scooped up a big bite of waffle. He put it in his mouth and started to chew. Lila noticed that he kept chewing for what seemed like a long time. She took a bite and was mortified. The waffles were impossible to swallow. It was like trying to eat rubber. They just sat at the table chewing and smiling at each other. Finally, Robby got up and left the room with the waffle still in his mouth.

When he left the room, Lila spit the waffle into her napkin. *What went wrong?* she thought to herself. *I followed every detail of the recipe. This is terrible. Now Robby's going to know I was lying about my cooking ability. Maybe he'll think I was lying about my whole orphan story.*

When Robby came back to the table, he took a big drink of water. He ate some of the strawberries and put down his fork. "I'm not so hungry for some reason," he said sweetly.

"I'm so sorry," Lila said, practically in tears. "These turned out to be a total disaster. I usually make great waffles. Maybe it's because I used a new recipe."

"Don't worry about it," Robby said. "That happens sometimes when you use a recipe you're not used to. Why don't we head out to the mall and get a bite there?"

"That's a great idea," Lila said. *And cooking waffles was definitely a terrible idea! Why did I ever get myself into this mess in the first place? What if he wants me to cook something else for him? I'm doomed!*

"So which color do you all like the best? Blushing pink or azalea red?" Sue asked. Sue, Jessica, and Elizabeth were at the beauty parlor having a manicure and pedicure for the wedding. "I think black would look nice," Jessica said, picking up a bottle of black polish from the manicurist's tray. "It would be different. A little funky. I'm sure Jeremy would love it."

Jessica stuck her tongue out at Elizabeth, who sent her a disapproving look, then she flashed a big smile at Sue.

"You do have a strange sense of humor," Sue said, laughing. "It's so—" Sue seemed unsure about how to end the sentence.

"Morbid and sick?" Elizabeth asked, glaring at her sister.

"No, just different," Sue said, smiling sweetly at Jessica. "I like it. I haven't been making a lot of jokes myself lately, so I'm glad someone else is."

"So, is this the first time you've ever had a manicure?" Jessica asked, trying to change the subject. Jessica certainly wasn't in the mood to have Sue compliment her.

"Well, actually, I've only had one once before, but after I'm married I plan on having a weekly manicure and massage," Sue said. "When we have a little more money, that is."

Jessica looked at Sue and couldn't help thinking that a weekly manicure and massage seemed awfully extravagant for someone who was supposed to be so outdoorsy and nature loving.

"You two really are the greatest for coming around with me today," Sue said.

"We wouldn't have missed spending your special day with you for anything," Elizabeth said, looking at Jessica. "Right, Jess?"

"Oh, of course," Jessica said sarcastically.

Sue obviously didn't pick up on the sarcasm in Jessica's tone. "I can't tell you how much it means to me that the two of you are going to walk down the aisle with me today. I feel like you're the sisters I never had. I'm also so glad that you've gotten to know Jeremy. I want you two to feel like we're both a part of your family from here on out."

"We're thrilled to be your bridesmaids," Elizabeth said. "It's going to be such a wonderful wedding."

179

Sue's smile dissolved into a weak frown. "I also really appreciate the fact that you didn't say anything to your parents about me being sick. I just didn't want them to worry."

Sue's sweetness was grating on Jessica's nerves. She was just a little too syrupy for Jessica's taste. Maybe she was being sincere, but it was still totally annoying. Jessica knew she should probably feel guilty about Jeremy but she wouldn't allow herself to. After all, it was Sue who was taking Jeremy away from the woman he truly loved. Sue was the one who was being selfish, she told herself. And she was certainly looking awfully radiant and perky for a dying woman.

"Ouch!" Sue pulled her hand away from the manicurist. "Where did you learn how to do nails? You're not supposed to prick your clients, for goodness sakes!" Sue's face turned bright red, and her tone was terse and commanding.

The manicurist apologized profusely and looked as though she was about to burst into tears.

This was the first time Jessica had seen this side of Sue's personality. It seemed so out of character for the sweet, innocent Sue that Jessica had come to know. *Well, maybe she has a little spunk in her after all,* Jessica thought. Jessica looked over at Elizabeth, who seemed just as startled by Sue's behavior as she was.

"Forgive me," Sue said, regaining her composure and putting her hand in the little bowl to soak it. "I don't know what came over me. I guess I must just be having a case of pre-wedding jitters." She turned to smile at Jessica and Elizabeth.

Jessica wondered if Jeremy had ever seen this side of Sue before. He would probably be mortified if he'd been there. Jeremy was so kind and patient with everyone. *Poor Jeremy*, Jessica thought to herself. *He probably has no idea what he's getting into.*

"Look at that adorable outfit!" Sue squealed as they passed by the window of Lizette's, one of the nicest clothing stores in Sweet Valley. "Would you mind if we just stopped in there for a minute so I could try it on? I still haven't found the perfect thing to wear when I leave the reception."

"Are you sure we have enough time?" Elizabeth asked. "The wedding's in just a few hours." Elizabeth looked at her watch. Even though she was trying not to worry about things so much, she couldn't help thinking that they should be home helping her mother get everything ready.

"It'll just take a minute, and besides, nothing calms my nerves like a little shopping," Sue said.

Elizabeth and Jessica sat down in the waiting area in front of the dressing rooms while Sue tried on the outfit.

"So, how do I look?" Sue walked out of the dressing room and modeled the beautiful designer suit.

"It's definitely you," Elizabeth said. "It's the perfect going-away dress."

"Oh, I'm so glad you think so," Sue said excitedly. "Now I'm going to try on some other things for the honeymoon. I'll be right back with the next gorgeous outfit, so don't go away."

Jessica turned to Elizabeth and whispered urgently. "Did you happen to see the price tag on that dress?" Jessica asked.

"No, why? Did you?"

"Yes, I did, as a matter of fact," Jessica said. "Guess how much it costs?"

"I really don't know and I really don't think it's any of our business anyway," Elizabeth said curtly.

"Just guess," Jessica pleaded.

"Oh, good grief." Elizabeth sighed. "I'll guess around two hundred dollars. So what?"

"Try one thousand dollars!" Jessica said excitedly. "Can you believe that? I thought when she gave it to the saleswoman to put in her dressing room that she was only trying it on for fun. I had no idea she was actually going to buy it!"

Elizabeth was trying to act like the price didn't really interest her, but inside she was thinking it was pretty surprising. Elizabeth reasoned that if *she* wasn't going to be alive for much longer, she would probably buy whatever she wanted. *Why shouldn't Sue have something special to wear on her big day?*

"Ta da!" Sue strode back out like a fashion model to show off a tight-fitting purple silk dress. "Isn't this the most delicious dress you've ever seen? Feel how soft it is," Sue commanded.

Elizabeth and Jessica took turns feeling the material. Elizabeth noticed that when it was Jessica's turn, she glanced at the price tag that was hanging off the sleeve.

"That's really pretty but I thought you guys were backpacking in the mountains on your honeymoon," Jessica said snidely.

Can't you just keep your mouth shut? Elizabeth wanted to yell at her twin. *You can't control her. You can't control her*, Elizabeth kept telling herself. That had become her new mantra since last night, but she had a feeling it was going to be harder to stick by that as the day went on and the wedding approached.

"I'm sure we'll have at least one occasion to go out for a nice meal somewhere," Sue said. "I like to be prepared for whatever comes along. And with Jeremy, I never know what to

183

expect. He's always full of surprises."

I can think of one that would really surprise you, Elizabeth thought. *In fact you'd be so surprised that you probably would think again about walking down that aisle in a few hours.*

"So, guess how much," Jessica said to Elizabeth once Sue had gone back to the dressing room.

"I don't care," Elizabeth said. She just wished Jessica would leave all this price stuff alone. As much as she didn't want it to, Sue's excessiveness was starting to bother her, too.

"Seven hundred dollars," Jessica blurted out. "I guess she's not only interested in trees and grass. I think diamonds and pearls are about the only things she cares about preserving."

"Will you cut it out?" Elizabeth snapped. "Why shouldn't she indulge herself a little bit? It *is* her wedding day and she *is* dying. I think she has the right to buy anything she wants to today. And you better not say anything to her to make her feel bad about the money she's spending. After all, it's not as if you're Miss Bargain Shopper when you buy a new outfit every time you have a date."

"I'm glad to see Miss Boss Everybody Around is back!" Jessica retorted. "What happened to your new policy of minding your own business and not bothering everyone with your sermons?"

Jessica was right. Elizabeth had broken her rule about not trying to control Jessica. *It was just a little slip up*, Elizabeth told herself. *But you better not push me again, Jessica Wakefield!*

Chapter 15

Jessica sat on her bed in her bridesmaid dress. Even though it was a peach-colored sheath, she felt as if she was wearing a black mourning dress. *I feel like I'm going to a funeral instead of a wedding. When Jeremy says, "I do," I know that a part of both of us is going to die.*

She could hear the noises downstairs of people running around to get ready for the wedding. The caterers were setting up for the reception, and Jessica could smell the food cooking in the kitchen. Out-of-town guests were dropping their belongings off, and it seemed as if the doorbell was ringing every five minutes with a different delivery.

Jessica knew that Sue was down the hall in her room, putting on her wedding dress.

Elizabeth had tried to get Jessica to help get Sue ready, saying it was a bridesmaid's responsibility. That was one thing Jessica couldn't get herself to do. It was bad enough that she had to walk down the aisle—she didn't have to help make the bride beautiful, too.

The sense of doom inside Jessica was darker and heavier than anything she'd ever felt before. She felt like the four walls were closing in on her. She looked around at all her things that used to give her so much pleasure—her CD player, her photographs, her posters, old love letters, and dried roses and corsages from dates past—but they all seemed completely meaningless. It wasn't just about being sad. She'd been sad a million times. This was different. She felt as if her whole world was collapsing. She didn't feel like she'd ever look forward to anything again. She couldn't imagine ever laughing or caring about the things she used to care about. For years, all she'd cared about was being popular and buying terrific clothes and having all the guys like her. Now, all those things seemed silly and unimportant.

In the past, whenever she wanted something—she somehow managed to get it. Even if something seemed impossible, she found a way to get around whatever obstacles were in her path. Jeremy was the one thing she wanted more than anything else she'd ever wanted in the world. And it was the one thing she couldn't have.

I guess the days of getting what I want are over now, she thought, sighing heavily. *So long to the Jessica Wakefield who could conquer the world. Hello to the Jessica Wakefield who's defeated and alone.*

"You look fabulous," Robby said, his eyes popping open as Lila opened the door and stood there in a raw silk, ivory sleeveless dress that showed off her terrific figure. Her brown hair was done up on her head in a turn-of-the-century bun, and she was covered in jewels. "You're going to steal the show from the bride."

"Thanks," Lila said, blushing. "You look pretty great yourself." He did look gorgeous. His brown hair and blue eyes were more striking than ever in contrast to the white tuxedo he was wearing.

Lila looked at Robby and realized how much she really cared for him. She'd never felt so strongly about anyone in the past. After brunch that morning, she'd decided to tell him the truth about her wealth. She just couldn't carry on with the charade any longer. She was consumed with fear as she realized that, in a few moments, he might be gone from her life completely.

"Robby, can you come inside for a minute? There's something I want to show you."

"Are you sure the Fowlers won't mind?" Robby asked as he walked hesitantly into the gigantic entrance hall and looked up at the expansive crystal chandelier hanging from the ceiling.

"I'm sure they won't mind," Lila said timidly.

"This is some place the Fowlers have," Robby said as they walked past the numerous rooms that opened onto the hallway. "It must be like living in a museum."

Lila led Robby up the stairs to her bedroom. "This is what I wanted to show you." She opened the door to her closet, which was the size of an average living room. It was filled with the most beautiful clothes imaginable, and dozens of pairs of shoes lined one entire wall.

"Is this the Fowlers' daughter's closet?" Robby asked, wide-eyed.

Lila looked at Robby and sighed. "No, this is my closet."

"Are all of these hand-me-downs?" Robby asked, confused.

"Robby, I have to confess something to you." Lila's voice was shaking and she felt a sharp pain in her stomach. "I've been lying to you."

"Lying about what?" Robby asked. "You look so upset. What could be so horrible?"

"I really am wealthy," she admitted. "I'm not

an orphan. I'm Lila Fowler, the one and only child of the Fowlers. Both of my parents are alive and healthy. All these clothes were bought first-hand for me. I've never cooked in my life except for those disgusting waffles I made for you this morning."

"I don't understand," Robby said, looking around the closet at all the clothes and shoes.

"I was so mad about you lying to me about being something you weren't that I wanted to give you a taste of your own medicine. Also, I was afraid that maybe you only liked me because I was wealthy. I thought maybe you were just using me for my money."

"But how could you think that?" Robby said. "I'm crazy about you."

"I know that now," Lila said. "I couldn't believe it when you didn't seem to mind that I was poor. But then I was afraid that you liked me more because you thought I was poor, and I thought you wouldn't like me if you thought I was rich. If you never want to see me again, I'll totally understand."

Robby pulled Lila close to him and held her in his arms. "Lila, don't you get it? I don't care if you're a princess or a pauper. All that matters to me is what's in there," Robby said, pointing to her forehead. Robby kissed her on the lips. "But do me one favor," he said when they came up for

191

air. "Just promise you'll leave the cooking to me from now on."

"It's a promise," Lila said as she started to leave the closet. "And promise me that the next time we go out to dinner, you won't order the most expensive dish and wine."

"I only did that to impress you," Robby said. "I thought you'd like it if I seemed to have expensive tastes."

"Oh, there is one more thing I should tell you," Lila said.

"I'm afraid to ask."

"I never wrote a poem in my life," Lila confessed. "In fact, I don't really like poetry that much."

"I plan on spending lots of time with you in the future, and I promise you I'll change your mind about that."

I wouldn't count on it, she thought. "It's a deal," Lila said. "Now, I believe we have a wedding to go to!"

The guests sat on white folding chairs on the beach, facing the water. The sun was setting on the ocean, and the light was soft with shades of pink and orange. A string quartet played Handel's "Water Music" and Jessica wanted to die. She kept biting the inside of her mouth to keep herself from bursting into tears.

"Go ahead," Elizabeth whispered urgently to Jessica. "It's your time to go now."

Jessica just stood there motionless. "Ouch!" she yelped as Elizabeth kicked her in the leg. "OK, OK, I'll go, but I want you to know that this is the hardest thing I've ever done in my entire life," Jessica said to her sister as she looked down the aisle at the man she loved.

Jeremy looked so uncomfortable standing up front by the altar in his tuxedo. He certainly didn't look like a man who was about to get married to the woman he loved. He looked more handsome than ever. *Why does he have to look so gorgeous today of all days? It just makes it even more unbearable.*

Jessica took the first few steps down the aisle and she caught Jeremy's gaze. She stood in her tracks until she heard her sister urging her on from behind. Jeremy's and Jessica's eyes were locked together as she continued her slow, painful walk.

Jessica heard the quartet start playing the wedding march when she reached the front of the aisle, and she saw all the heads turn toward Sue. Sue's image was a blur to Jessica. It was almost as if she couldn't see her. All Jessica could see was a cloud of white floating down the aisle, on the arm of Sue's stepfather. She felt a sharp pain shooting into her chest. She didn't know how she would be able to continue to stand there throughout the ceremony.

All the moments she had shared with Jeremy flashed before her. She felt like she was standing on the beach alone. It was as if all the people had suddenly disappeared.

She was standing almost exactly at the same spot where she'd seen Jeremy for the first time. The sound of the waves and the smell of the salt air were exactly as they'd been on that magical day. When she first laid her eyes on him, she knew she had found her destiny. She wondered if Jeremy was remembering that moment now.

As Sue approached the altar, her face finally came into Jessica's focus. Jessica had a realization that was more crystal clear than anything she'd ever thought before. *She is the wrong woman for him! His life is going to be miserable! My life is going to be miserable! I won't let her ruin our lives like that! The old Jessica Wakefield isn't ready to be laid to rest yet! The real Jessica Wakefield would never surrender to this horrible fate! Hello, Jessica! Watch out, world! I'm back!*

Elizabeth was so nervous as she stood next to Jessica that she could feel her hands trembling. *Please behave yourself*, Elizabeth silently begged her twin. *Don't spoil this moment for*

Sue! This could be one of the last happy moments of Sue's life.

It seemed to Elizabeth that it was taking Father Bishop forever to get through the ceremony. He was reading a story from the Bible that seemed like the longest story Elizabeth had ever heard. *Just get on with it, Father*, she almost blurted out. She wished he would just skip over all that other stuff and get to the part where he said, "I now pronounce you husband and wife."

Elizabeth looked at Sue, who was beaming wildly at Jeremy. She looked so pale and fragile yet happy and hopeful. Elizabeth was thinking how stunning Sue looked in her wedding dress—the same dress that Jessica had tried to destroy.

Elizabeth wanted Sue's final years to be the happiest years of her life. She hoped that Jeremy would be loyal and kind to his bride, even if he wasn't in love with her. Elizabeth wondered for a moment if maybe she should have told Sue the truth about Jeremy. It was too late now, anyway, and it would only hurt her more to know the truth. It wasn't as if she had to spend a whole lifetime with him, after all. Unfortunately, Sue's lifetime was almost over. Elizabeth knew that if Sue weren't sick, she would have told Sue everything.

As the sun continued to set, the colors in the sky became even deeper and more brilliant. Elizabeth had never seen a more beautiful sunset. The beauty of the ceremony seemed almost cruel to Elizabeth in contrast to Sue's illness.

"Marriage is a sacrament that should not be entered into lightly," Father Bishop continued. "It is a blessed coming together of a man and a woman who have decided to take the miraculous journey of life together. . . ."

Elizabeth turned her gaze toward Jeremy and saw something that caused her heart to constrict. He wasn't looking at Sue! He was gazing into the eyes of Jessica! *How could he? At his own wedding!* To make matters worse, Sue grabbed Jeremy's hand and seemed to be trying desperately to direct his wandering eyes toward her own. Elizabeth looked at Jessica, whose eyes were planted firmly on Jeremy. She knew her sister well enough to know that she was trying to send some sort of terrible message to Jeremy.

Elizabeth didn't think her nerves could take much more of this. She looked in the front row at the smiling faces of her parents. They looked completely oblivious. As far as they knew, this was a wonderful moment. Never in their wildest dreams would they have been able to imagine what was really going on beneath the surface.

Suddenly, Elizabeth sensed Jessica's body tense

up. *Hurry up! Hurry up!* Elizabeth felt herself break into a sweat.

"If any man or woman knows of any reason why this couple should not be joined as one under the realm of God, speak now, or forever hold your peace."

Elizabeth held her breath and closed her eyes.

"I do!" Jessica shouted.

Elizabeth couldn't believe what she was hearing. Maybe she imagined it. She opened her eyes and saw the shocked expression on Father Bishop's face, and she knew her worst fears had come true.

"You do what?" Father Bishop asked. His voice was shaking.

"I know why they shouldn't be married," Jessica said as tears rolled down her face.

"And what might that reason be, my child?" Father Bishop asked as sweat formed on his brow and his neck turned red inside his clerical collar.

"Jeremy can't marry Sue because he's not in love with her," Jessica blurted out. The crowd seemed to all gasp in horror at the same time.

"What are you talking about?" Sue shouted at Jessica.

"It's the truth, Sue," Jessica said. "Jeremy's really in love with me."

"Jeremy?" Sue looked at Jeremy, anticipating a denial.

"Is this true?" Father Bishop asked Jeremy. "Are you in love with this young lady here?"

Jeremy looked at Sue and then at Father Bishop. "Yes, Father," he said sadly. "It's true."

"Well, then, that is that," Father Bishop pronounced. "This ceremony is officially void and null."

Everything had happened so quickly that Elizabeth could barely fathom what had transpired. In all their sixteen years, Jessica had never done anything so outrageous. Elizabeth was completely enraged. Her whole body shook with fury. Elizabeth looked at Sue, whose face had turned the color of her wedding dress. She watched as Robby caught Sue just as she was about to collapse to the ground.

"Jessica, how could you?" Mrs. Wakefield looked at Jessica with an expression of disgust that Elizabeth had never seen before. She ran over to Sue and hugged her with tears in her eyes.

All the guests were talking frantically and moving around in chaos and confusion. Elizabeth looked at Jessica, who was still standing where she'd been just a few moments before she'd created this disaster. Jessica was staring out at the ocean, and she looked as if she was in a trance.

Elizabeth grabbed Jessica's arm and led her to the Jeep. As she turned around, she saw

Father Bishop lead Jeremy down the beach—
away from the crowd and the wreckage of the
wedding that never happened.

*Don't miss two tantalizing new Sweet Valley
High Magnas, Elizabeth's Secret Diary and
Jessica's Secret Diary. Read about Elizabeth's
forbidden love affair and Jessica's taboo kiss!*

*Then, Jeremy is back in Sweet Valley High
#109, Double-crossed!, the first book in the new
three-part miniseries, Sweet Valley Scandal.
Sweet Valley has never been so shocked!*

Bantam Books in the Sweet Valley High series
Ask your bookseller for the books you have missed

SIGN UP FOR THE SWEET VALLEY HIGH® FAN CLUB!

Hey, girls! Get all the gossip on Sweet Valley High's® most popular teenagers when you join our fantastic Fan Club! As a member, you'll get all of this really cool stuff:

- Membership Card with your own personal Fan Club ID number
- A Sweet Valley High® Secret Treasure Box
- Sweet Valley High® Stationery
- Official Fan Club Pencil (for secret note writing!)
- Three Bookmarks
- A "Members Only" Door Hanger
- Two Skeins of J. & P. Coats® Embroidery Floss with flower barrette instruction leaflet
- Two editions of *The Oracle* newsletter
- Plus exclusive Sweet Valley High® product offers, special savings, contests, and much more!

Be the first to find out what Jessica & Elizabeth Wakefield are up to by joining the Sweet Valley High® Fan Club for the one-year membership fee of only $6.25 each for U.S. residents, $8.25 for Canadian residents (U.S. currency). Includes shipping & handling.

Send a check or money order (do not send cash) made payable to "Sweet Valley High® Fan Club" along with this form to:

SWEET VALLEY HIGH® FAN CLUB, BOX 3919-B, SCHAUMBURG, IL 60168-3919

NAME _____
(Please print clearly)

ADDRESS _____

CITY _____ STATE _____ ZIP _____
(Required)

AGE _____ BIRTHDAY _____ / _____ / _____

Offer good while supplies last. Allow 6-8 weeks after check clearance for delivery. Addresses without ZIP codes cannot be honored. Offer good in USA & Canada only. Void where prohibited by law.
©1993 by Francine Pascal   LCI-1383-123